Praise for
GORDON KORMAN

Slacker

"Highly entertaining, upbeat, inspiring, and full of
Korman's signature sense of humor."
—*Publishers Weekly*

"An excellent pick for reluctant readers."
—*School Library Journal*

Swindle

"Scary, funny, and hysterical adventures!"
—*Chicago Tribune*

The Hypnotists

"Fast-paced. . . . An entertaining mix of intense
action and goofy fun." —*Publishers Weekly*

Ungifted

"A gem for readers looking for a story where the
underdog comes out on top." —*VOYA*

Schooled

★ "This rewarding novel features an engaging main
character and some memorable moments of comedy,
tenderness, and reflection." —*Booklist*, starred review

Look for more action and humor from

GORDON KORMAN

The Hypnotists series
The Hypnotists
Memory Maze
The Dragonfly Effect

The Swindle series
Swindle
Zoobreak
Framed
Showoff
Hideout
Jackpot
Unleashed
Jingle

The Titanic trilogy

The Kidnapped trilogy

The On the Run series

The Dive trilogy

The Everest trilogy

The Island trilogy

Restart

Radio Fifth Grade

The Toilet Paper Tigers

The Chicken Doesn't Skate

This Can't Be Happening at Macdonald Hall!

GORDON KORMAN

slacker

SCHOLASTIC INC.

Copyright © 2017 by Gordon Korman

This book was originally published in hardcover by Scholastic Press in 2016.

Published by Scholastic Inc., *Publishers since 1920*. SCHOLASTIC and associated logos are trademarks and/or registered trademarks of Scholastic Inc.

The publisher does not have any control over and does not assume any responsibility for author or third-party websites or their content.

No part of this publication may be reproduced, stored in a retrieval system, or transmitted in any form or by any means, electronic, mechanical, photocopying, recording, or otherwise, without written permission of the publisher. For information regarding permission, write to Scholastic Inc., Attention: Permissions Department, 557 Broadway, New York, NY 10012.

This book is a work of fiction. Names, characters, places, and incidents are either the product of the author's imagination or are used fictitiously, and any resemblance to actual persons, living or dead, business establishments, events, or locales is entirely coincidental.

ISBN 978-0-545-82316-6

10 9   19 20 21

Printed in the U.S.A.   40
First printing 2017

Book design by Nina Goffi

For Harry and Nancy Korman

CHAPTER ONE
CAMERON BOXER

It was ill—ill being a good thing for it to be.

The basement was dim. The couch was soft and comfortable, perfectly molded to the contours of my butt by the thousands of hours I'd spent on it. And the aliens coming out of the smoldering wreckage of the mothership were dazed and slow, ripe for the blasting.

It was a moment to savor, but there was no time for savoring. The controller was an extension of my hands as I took aim and fired. My friends Pavel and Chuck had my back, and also this guy Borje, who was in Malmo, Sweden. Their voices rang out through my headset. We were a tight-knit team, even though Pavel was playing from three doors down, Chuck from two blocks over, and Borje at a distance of five thousand miles. The aliens were shouting, too, but they didn't seem to be as organized as we were. And definitely not as dedicated.

I heard another voice—my mother's—coming from upstairs. I ignored it. Nothing that happened on Earth could be important right now.

The basement lights began to flash on and off. Now, that annoyed me. With great effort, I had created a cave-like atmosphere ideal for gaming. And here was Mom, standing outside the cave, flicking a switch and ruining my concentration.

"What?" I hollered, my finger tapping the Y control, which created a steady pulse of Omega radiation that the extraterrestrials were especially sensitive to.

Another thing my mother didn't understand: "What?" was not a real question. "What?" meant "I'm busy" or "Do not disturb" or even "Go shout at someone who isn't involved in a life-and-death struggle with seven-foot insects!"

She said something about having to go out, ziti in the oven, and ten minutes. What I heard was "blah, blah, blah, blah, blah, blah, blah." Seriously, if she was going to be back in ten minutes, why did I have to know about this at all? I had an alien hit squad on my tail.

I focused on the screen, trying to peer through the burning extraterrestrial atmosphere. Suddenly a voice eerily like Darth Vader's announced, "Cover me while I plant the heavy-neutron seed."

Chuck was the first to panic. "Cam! Did you hear that? It's him!"

"Yeah, but which one is he?" Pavel added desperately.

Borje was babbling excitedly, but when he got too amped up, he switched to Swedish, so he wasn't much help.

I stared at the hideous aliens on the screen, with their

armored, insectoid bodies; undulating antennae; and cold, hooded eyes. It was impossible to tell which was being manipulated by the owner of that deep voice.

I screamed one word: *"Attack!"*

And we did, blasting away with lasers, disruptors, and antimatter grenades. I even threw rocks. It had to be the most intense battle we'd ever fought. It raged on and on and on. Pavel had to leave to eat dinner, and Borje's dad caught him and made him go to bed. It was just me and Chuck against a lone enemy, holed up in the wreckage of his escape pod. We had him cornered, but you couldn't tell by the way he was fighting, firing at us through a breach in the strontium field.

"You'll never reach me in here!" the deep voice leered.

Of course, we should have expected that the last alien standing would be him. The gamer with the Darth Vader voice synthesizer had been stalking me online for months, foiling my Normandy invasions, sacking my quarterbacks, forcing my chariots out of the Circus Maximus, and battering me with steel chairs in extreme wrestling matches. I didn't even know the guy's name—not his real one, anyway. He went by his gamer tag, Evil McKillPeople, of Toronto, Canada. My archnemesis.

"What are we going to do, Cam?" Chuck was losing his nerve. "We can't blast through strontium!"

"Aim for the breach!" I advised.

"But *he's* aiming at *us*! And—Oh, hi, Mom. Dinnertime already?"

"Do not put down that controller!" I ordered. "We've got him outnumbered!"

The next voice I heard wasn't Chuck's or Darth Vader's. It seemed to be coming from outside. What was it saying? I raised the headphones from my ears.

"This is the Sycamore Fire Department. Is there anybody in the house?"

Well, that had to be the stupidest question ever asked. Of course I was in the house. Why did the fire department want to know that?

Without putting down the controller, I got up, ran to the high window, yanked away the pillow I'd jammed there for extra darkness, and peered outside. All I could see were fire engines and guys in heavy raincoats and rubber boots.

"What?" I exclaimed aloud, and this time it didn't mean "Do not disturb" or "I'm busy." It meant: "Why is the entire Sycamore Fire Department parked on our lawn?"

An enormous crash shook the foundation of the house. Heavy running footfalls sounded upstairs. A moment later, the basement door was flung wide and one of those giant raincoats appeared on the stairs, enveloped in a thick cloud of smoke.

"Kid, what are you doing here?" he barked.

"I'm finally going to beat Evil McKillPeople!" I yelled back.

"Your house is on fire!"

He shoved me upstairs, the controller still clutched in my hand. By that time, another firefighter had invaded the kitchen and found the baked ziti—a coal-black charred lump of carbon.

"False alarm," he announced. "This casserole burned and the whole house filled with smoke. Neighbor reported it pouring out the windows." He turned to me. "Good luck getting the black off the ceiling."

My mother's "blah, blah, blah, blah, blah, blah, blah" came back to me then. Only this time, it sounded more like "I'm making a baked ziti for dinner. Wait ten minutes and take it out of the oven."

That would probably have been about an hour ago— you know, back when our house still had a front door. I'd always wondered why firemen carry axes. Now I knew.

I was bound to hear a whole lot about this later tonight. It was definitely going to disturb my lifestyle.

Worst of all, when I finally went back down to the basement, the TV screen showed my character lying stone-dead on the alien surface. Evil McKillPeople was standing over him, a leering grin on his green lips.

Video games were exactly like life, only better.

Both followed the laws of cause and effect. You take a turn too fast in a racing game, you roll your car. Or in the real world, if you don't hear your mom talking about ziti in the oven, the fire department will bust down your door.

It was easy to get a new race car. That happened with the touch of a button on your controller. Our door, on the other hand, turned out to be a nonstandard size.

"Fensterman says it's going to take a month to custom-make a new one!" raved my father, explaining why we now lived with a piece of plywood nailed across the front entrance of our house. For the next month, we would have to use the back door.

Dad wasn't shouting because he was mad at me. He was shouting to be heard over the roar of the giant fans that stood all around, blowing out the smoke and burnt smell left over from the ziti.

He also happened to be mad at me. Just not as mad as Mom.

"I asked one little thing of you, Cameron Boxer," she seethed. "One thing: Take out the ziti after ten minutes and turn off the oven."

"That's two things," I pointed out.

"Two things any orangutan could do, no problem!" she raged. "Of course, he'd have to swing away from the game console for thirty seconds."

Now, that bothered me. "You know," I said, "you and Dad run a furniture store because that's your lifestyle. Video games are *my* lifestyle. I'm not a big furniture fan, but I don't dump all over it, because I respect your lifestyle."

My father's eyes bulged. "That 'lifestyle' puts food on the table and clothes on your back. And it pays for things like video games and the electricity to run them."

"First prize at Rule the World is ten thousand dollars," I reminded them. That was the East Coast gaming championship coming up in November. Pavel, Chuck, and I were in training—although I hadn't decided yet which of those guys to take on as my wingman. We called ourselves the Awesome Threesome, but Rule the World only accepted twosomes.

Mom sighed. "It's not the money. It's not the dinner. It's not even the house full of smoke and the ruined door."

"It's a little bit about the door," Dad corrected her. "And it'll be a little more if our insurance premium goes up because of this."

Mom ignored him. "Look at yourself, Cam. You're pale as a ghost. You look like you just got out of prison. The best thing I can say about your grades is that you're not failing. You've never played a sport—"

"Too sweaty," I interjected.

She forged on. "Or did drama—"

"Too showy."

"Or joined a club—"

"Too many strangers."

"Or participated in a single extracurricular activity. Cam, if you didn't have a birth certificate, it would be next to impossible to prove that you even exist! Your only interest is video games."

She said this like it was a bad thing. I was proud of my lifestyle. I saw this guy on TV once who said the key to happiness was to find what you love to do, and do it. I'd lived by that rule for every one of my thirteen years. Obviously, I still went to school, and flossed, and got haircuts and flu shots and all that. Even the TV guy admitted nobody could get away with only the good stuff. But if you could keep the balance in favor of doing what you love—80–20, let's say—you could be at least 80 percent happy. Which was still pretty ill.

My dad took up the lecture. "We're not saying there's anything wrong with video games in moderation. But you don't do anything else. Sooner or later it's going to cost you the chance to have any kind of life that doesn't come with an avatar on a screen. Not to mention that you're hogging the game system that was bought for the whole family. Your poor sister has to go to a friend's house if she wants to play at all because you're always on ours."

"Melody's not a serious gamer like me," I defended myself. "I'm in training. Doesn't that show initiative and involvement?"

Dad took a deep breath. "Listen up, kid. First of all, we're going to be using the back door for the next month. In that time, you will find something else to be interested in besides video games. It can be a sport; it can be a club; it can be anything you want, so long as it involves real human beings and it doesn't happen on a screen."

I was horrified. "But what about Rule the World? I've been practicing for months!"

Mom spoke up. "We're not taking your games away. Yet. But we're not kidding, Cameron. Your life is going to change."

"Is it the ziti?" I demanded. "It's the ziti, right? When I win the contest, I'll buy you ten thousand dollars' worth of ziti!"

"Don't be ridiculous. Your future is more important than any amount of ziti. This is going to happen, Cameron. It's going to happen before we have a real door again. And if it doesn't, you *will* lose that game system."

I staggered back. Honestly—like I'd been punched.

I remembered something else the TV guy had mentioned: There were always going to be people trying to mess up your lifestyle.

I'd been on guard for those people my entire life. But I never dreamed they'd turn out to be my own parents.

CHAPTER TWO
PAVEL DYSAN

Technically, Cam hadn't chosen me yet as his Rule the World partner. But it was coming any day now. For starters, I was tops in the entire eighth grade in academic average. Oh, sure, school smarts didn't necessarily translate into video-gaming skills. But problem solving was a big part of it. Also logic and quick thinking. What more could anybody ask for in a wingman?

It wasn't so much that I was *better* than Chuck, just more levelheaded. I could play myself out of any tight spot. When Chuck got himself backed into a corner, he'd panic and do something crazy. Nine times out of ten, he'd get himself killed, and we'd lose a life, or spend health points, or waste time waiting for him to respawn. That wasn't the kind of guy you'd want as your partner in real competition.

Mind you, every now and then, by sheer random chance, Chuck would go nuts on his controller and wipe out the enemy single-handed. If Cam was thinking about one of *those* times, he might get it in his head to pick Chuck over me. I'd be happy for him, and I'd still cheer for them at Rule the World. But I'd be wasting my time, because they'd definitely lose.

And now there was this other problem.

Technically, you couldn't blame Mr. and Mrs. Boxer for being ticked off. Cam could have burned their whole house down, and himself with it. As it was, every room smelled like a luau gone out of control, and the kitchen cabinets and ceiling were all black.

But banning Cam from gaming was like telling Bill Gates to give up computers and count on his fingers! There'd be no Rule the World for any of us. Regardless of whether the partner ended up being me or Chuck, there was never any question that the main guy was always Cam.

"What are you going to do?" I asked him the day after the Great Ziti Inferno.

He shrugged, dangling a long gummy worm and directing it into his upturned mouth. "My parents say I have to get involved. Show initiative—whatever that's supposed to mean."

I provided the definition: "Initiative is the drive or ambition to get something done."

Chuck looked worried. "We're dead. Nobody has less of that than Cam."

"I have initiative," Cam defended himself. "It takes a lot of work to do as little as I've done for the past thirteen years."

The three of us were in our usual after-school haunt—Sweetness and Light, the only candy store left in Sycamore now that everything had moved out to the new mall. Cam was positive that gummy worms were a kind of brain food that made you sharper at video games. (The science behind that was technically zero.)

"We can kiss that ten thousand bucks good-bye," Chuck pronounced darkly.

"Not necessarily," I countered. "Cam's folks want him to get involved. So all he has to do is join something."

Cam flinched, and a gummy worm bounced off his cheek and hit the floor of the little shop. "I thought of that," he admitted. "The problem is, when you join something, they expect you to do it. To"—he shuddered—"*participate*. Man, I hate that word."

"Yeah," I challenged, "but if it's the only way to save Rule the World . . ."

"You don't understand," he persisted. "Let's say I join the soccer team. I'd have practice every day and go to games on the weekend. Or drama. They're always rehearsing and performing. Even the chess club—can you see me waiting twenty minutes for some guy to make a move? None of that stuff fits into my lifestyle!"

"*I'm* in the chess club," I reminded him. School champion, two years running.

Chuck was in true pain. "You can't just give up!"

"Listen," said Cam. "Some people knock themselves out for straight A's—"

"*I* get straight A's," I protested.

"Yeah, but it's *normal* for you to get straight A's, just like it's normal for me to just squeak by. Some people play sports, or jump out of airplanes, or climb mountains. I *could* do those things, but it wouldn't be *me*. It would be some guy who cares about that stuff."

I took a bite of gummy worm, but the candy turned to acid in my mouth. (Take it from a guy who actually understood the chemical process behind that.) A lot of words had been used to describe Cameron Boxer over the years— *goof-off, loafer, shiftless, slouch, lazy blob of protoplasm.* Those all said it pretty well, but he was more than that, too. What people couldn't see was that there was something special about Cam. Yes, he was a slacker. But Cam was a slacker the way LeBron James was a basketball player— through a mixture of rare natural gift and intense practice.

I spun my stool around and peered through the plate-glass window of the shop. Main Street was normally quiet since the Sycamore Mall had opened, but now the road was clogged with high school kids, soaking wet and covered in what looked like soap suds.

"What's going on out there?" I asked Mrs. Bachman, who owned Sweetness and Light.

The storekeeper followed my gaze, scowling. "Those Friends of Fuzzy! Washing cars, they are!"

Secretly, we referred to Mrs. B as Mrs. Backward, because that's how she said everything. As in, "Gummy worms, you boys want?"

I was surprised she was so down on the Friends of Fuzzy, who were really famous in our town for doing good things like fund-raising and charity work. They operated out of Sycamore High. The name came from the high school's mascot, Farley J. Peachfuzz.

Foam-spattered teenagers moved among the passing vehicles, dancing and trying to wave drivers onto the shoulder, where even foamier kids waited with sponges and buckets.

A large banner was strung between two light poles:

1ST ANNUAL CAR WASH FOR SPLEEN HEALTH
CLEAN CAR, HEALTHY SPLEEN

Well, I didn't know the difference between a healthy spleen and an unhealthy one. (I made a mental note to Google it, though.) But it sure didn't seem like the kind of thing anyone could be against.

Chuck thought so, too. "What's wrong with the Friends of Fuzzy? Everybody likes the things they do."

"Blocking traffic, those kids," Mrs. B said disapprovingly. "An honest living, I'm trying to earn."

"It's for a good cause—I think," I offered.

She snorted. "Ruining people's livelihoods—such a good cause! Some advice, I'll give you—don't get involved."

All at once, Cam snapped to attention. I'd seen that expression on his face before—when he'd found the cheat code on this shady Korean website that got us a free combat prestige upgrade. But nothing like that was happening now.

Then it came to me. Mrs. B had just said the magic word: *involved*.

Chuck didn't pick up on it. "Oh, we're not allowed in the Friends of Fuzzy," he told the storekeeper. "It's just for high school. We're in eighth grade."

"But what if someone started something like the Friends of Fuzzy at our school?" Cam asked.

I regarded him warily. "Like who?"

"Like me."

Chuck was completely baffled. "What are you talking about?"

I thought I knew, but surely I had it wrong.

Mrs. B sounded suspicious. "The street, you won't be blocking?"

Cam laughed. "I guarantee you've got nothing to worry about!"

I had a sinking feeling that the head worrier was about to be me.

Computers were another one of my talents. I'd first hacked into the school's website before lunch on day one of sixth grade.

Cam peered over my shoulder. "Open up a new page under 'School Clubs.'"

We'd gone straight from Sweetness and Light to my house—more specifically, to the laptop in my basement.

"I don't get it," I told him, poised at the keyboard. "If you want to convince your folks you're getting involved, sign up for the film club and sleep in the dark. How could it be easier to start a middle school Friends of Fuzzy?"

"I'll join," Chuck offered loyally.

"No, you won't," Cam promised, "because this isn't a real club. Don't you get it? We create this splashy web page about a group of do-gooders and the amazing ways we serve the citizens of Sycamore. We make it sound like, compared to us, the Friends of Fuzzy are all goof-offs who wouldn't give anybody else the skin off a grape. We're dedicated, motivated, community-minded! And here's the most important part: We don't do any of it. We just *say* we do it."

Chuck looked dazed. "What's the point of a club that isn't a club?"

"When my folks try to ban me from gaming, I'll show them the page. Not only did I join something—I started it. I'm the president."

It was a great idea, an *inspired* idea, even—doing less by pretending to do more. For all my appearances on the honor roll, I could never have come up with a scheme like that.

Still, I wouldn't have been a true friend if I didn't let him know I had my doubts. "What if it doesn't work?"

He was dumbfounded. "How could it not work?"

"Well, first of all, your parents might not believe it," I began.

"Why won't they believe it? It's on the school's website. Why would the school lie?"

I chose my words carefully. "Your folks might think it's a little too good to be true that you went from zero to running the show just like that. Or maybe the school will figure out that it's all a hoax. Then not only will *you* be in trouble, but the whole thing can be traced to *my* computer."

"The school never looks at their website except to post snow days," he countered. "And my parents will be so overjoyed I'm getting involved in something besides video games that they'll never question it. They *deserve* to be happy, considering all their business worries. Who are we to mess with their happiness?"

He was right about the business worries. Sweetness and Light wasn't the only store in town that was suffering because of the mall. Boxer's Furniture Showroom was losing a lot of customers to the big new department stores.

I sighed. "Fine. Does this wonderful club have a name?"

"How about Friends of Fuzzy, Junior?" Chuck suggested.

Cam shook his head seriously. "If we connect ourselves to *them*, we might be expected to help out with *their* stuff. If we have to do anything, the whole point of the club is down the tubes. No, we have to keep it general. How about the Positive Action Group?"

I typed it onto the web page. I couldn't explain why, but it looked pretty good up there on the screen—like it stood for everything, when really it meant nothing at all. We might as well have called it Harry.

"It's—okay," I admitted in grudging surprise.

"It's perfect," Chuck added reverently.

"Ill," Cam agreed.

We got to work—not technically something you said very often when "we" included Cam. It took some doing, but when I pushed my swivel chair back from the computer, the result on the screen was well worth it.

POSITIVE ACTION GROUP

"Because helping others is an education in itself."

MISSION STATEMENT: The mission of the Positive Action Group is to act positively to help our school and our community. We pledge to be positive and never negative, because negative actions are worse than no actions at all. We look forward to a fantastic year of helping.

MEET CAMERON BOXER, P.A.G. PRESIDENT: Cam is an eighth grader at Sycamore Middle School. He got the idea for the Positive Action Group when he noticed that all the other clubs were about games or sports or activities, but none were about helping. And so, the P.A.G. was born.

CLICK HERE TO CONTACT CAM

"It's awesome—except for that last part," Cam told me. "I don't want anybody contacting me. I'm doing this so I can be left alone."

"That's the beauty of it," I said smugly. I clicked the mouse, and instantly another page appeared on top of the first one.

WEBSITE UNDER CONSTRUCTION

The P.A.G. asks for your patience as we think of even more kind and unselfish ways to help out. We will be back up and running before you know it.

"Wow," Cam said with raised eyebrows.

I glowed. There was something about pleasing Cam. He was the kind of guy you wanted to impress, even though you knew the feeling wasn't mutual. Cam didn't try to impress. That didn't make him a bad friend. It was just that impressing people didn't fit into his lifestyle. And, of course, that lifestyle was what made him Cam.

The people who looked down on Cam were technically missing the point. He wasn't just a slacker; he was the Leonardo da Vinci of slackers.

And the Positive Action Group might turn out to be his *Mona Lisa*.

CHAPTER THREE
DAPHNE LEIBOWITZ

I couldn't stop worrying about Elvis.

What was going to happen to him? Rejected by his whole family . . . kicked out of his home . . . wandering around town with no place to call his own. It was so tragic. I got choked up just thinking about it.

He was so adorable, too. Buck teeth, fat cheeks, flat tail. When he slapped the water, you could hear it half a mile away. But not anymore. There was no water left to slap—not since they drained the creek when they built the new mall. I bet it hurt to beat your tail against the tarmac of the parking lot.

He was too old to keep up, I guess. The rest of the beaver colony moved on when their lodge was destroyed by the construction company. But Elvis couldn't hack it, the poor little guy. He stayed behind in Sycamore and made the best of it. But he had *nothing*—no lodge, no other beavers to hang out with, no purpose in life besides chewing on things. He still did that. And when he chewed on people's fence posts and swing sets and deck chairs and cable wires, they got angry just because the TV went out during *Sunday Night Football*.

Those were the kinds of people who lived in this town: People who valued football over a human life. Well, a beaver life, anyway.

That was the whole problem with Sycamore. Nobody cared—not about a poor homeless beaver, not about anything. We all stood around, pretending everything was fine while the mall sucked all the business away from Main Street. No—it was worse than that. We were the customers abandoning our own town and driving to the mall to do our shopping. No wonder the Transportation Department was planning to demolish Sycamore's crumbling interstate exit, now that there was another ramp a mile and a half down the road to service the mall. Think about that: Our whole community wasn't worth the cost of a little shoring up and road work. What would happen to our stores then? For all anybody gave a hoot, they'd close one by one, leaving downtown an empty shell. And then poor Elvis wouldn't even have the garbage Dumpsters to eat out of.

Our school was a perfect example of Sycamore's bad attitude. I sat with my iPad, browsing through the Sycamore Middle website. There were pictures of parties, dances, and pep rallies. Even the listings of school clubs only emphasized how self-centered we were. The track team—oh, you can't run? Too bad. The art club—you're all thumbs? Take a hike. The drama society—you've got stage fright? Tough buns. The chess club—no brains? No dice.

And . . . what was this? The Positive Action Group? I'd never heard of that one before. It must have been something new. It was probably cheesy, but the name sounded so—positive.

I read the whole thing, and I'll bet my jaw was hanging down to my knees. Confession: I could be kind of a complainer. But the Positive Action Group wasn't just positive; it was exactly what Sycamore Middle School needed most—and at exactly the right time. In the middle of all these selfish teams and clubs designed to cry out, *"Look how great I am!"* here was a school organization completely devoted to helping other people.

I pictured the crowded halls between periods—eight hundred kids grunting, shoving, and slouching their way to the next class. Who in that group could possibly be awesome enough to have come up with the Positive Action Group?

I squinted at the screen:

MEET CAMERON BOXER, P.A.G. PRESIDENT

Cameron Boxer?

I knew Cam Boxer. He was the laziest kid in the whole school! There was no way he could be the head of anything like the P.A.G. *A* stood for *Action*, and he was the total opposite of that. The only helping he ever did was helping himself to cookies on Parents' Night.

But maybe I was wrong. People changed, after all. Like, I used to eat tuna that wasn't caught in dolphin-safe nets, and now I'd rather starve. Cam didn't seem like the kind of guy who'd get into helping people, but who was I to judge? After all, it was right here in black and white on the school's website.

He deserved my support, not my suspicion. The P.A.G. would never have a more enthusiastic member than me.

I wasn't even going to wait till Monday to join up. Since the contact link on the site wasn't working, I would go over to Cam's house this minute to sign on the dotted line. And it would be my chance to tell Cam face-to-face how great I thought he was for doing this.

I looked up his address. He lived on Ontario Street, only a few blocks over from me.

When I got there, it was kind of weird. The house was nice enough—two stories with red brick and white-painted shutters. But there was no door. It wasn't open, or anything like that. Where the door should have been, someone had nailed up a big sheet of plywood.

I knocked on it and called out, "Cam?"

There was no answer, although I could hear sounds coming from inside—kind of like distant explosions.

I banged harder. I couldn't find a doorbell—it might have been covered by the plywood. Quite a few people had scribbled their names on the surface. I knew some of them from school. Was this kind of like leaving a message, the plywood equivalent of voice mail? Was I supposed to do that, too?

I didn't. Writing on walls was almost like vandalism. For sure the Positive Action Group would be against that.

It was then that I noticed a light glimmering in the corner of a basement window. I crouched to peer inside. I couldn't see much because there was some kind of pillow jammed in the inside alcove. But through a tiny corner, I could squint into the rec room in the basement. This was definitely where the explosions were coming from. I could hear them much more clearly as I hunkered down in the flower bed. And there was Cam—or at least I thought it was him. I could only make out the top of his head, but it was his light brown hair and slightly hunched shoulders.

What was he doing down there? Why didn't he answer the door? I mean, there was no door, but why didn't he answer the plywood? I'd banged pretty hard.

This time I got down on my knees and knocked on the glass. The kid didn't even look up. I was starting to get a little worried. What chance did the Positive Action Group have if its president didn't know enough to answer his door—or whatever was supposed to be nailed across the front entrance of his house?

"*Cameron Boxer!!*" I bellowed.

CHAPTER FOUR
CAMERON BOXER

As the landing craft approached the shores of Okinawa, we were taking withering fire from the island's defenders. Shells burst all around us, sending up geysers of water. Tracer bullets cut through the waves. The thump of anti-aircraft guns assaulted my eardrums, sending black puffs into the sky above. And another sound—I lifted the headset from my ears and strained to hear.

Bang, rattle! . . . "Cameron Boxer!" . . . *Rattle, bang!*

"Who's making all that noise?" I asked in annoyance.

"It's the Japanese army!" called Chuck over the headset.

"Not *that* noise! Somebody's outside my house!"

"Don't look at us," Pavel reasoned. "How could we be in the game if we're outside your house?"

And then we all heard Darth Vader's diabolical cackle. Chuck panicked. "Evil McKillPeople!"

I used the controller to take evasive action. "He won't get us this time!"

There was a crimson flash and a deafening boom, and pieces of our boat and our avatar bodies began raining down into the sea. I distinctly saw my leg go by. For the first time, I found myself regretting that the graphics

28

in this war game were so realistic. Who was this Canadian, this Evil McKillPeople? And why was he so good that he could always wreck me?

Bang, rattle! . . . "Cameron Boxer!" . . . *Rattle, bang!*

I glanced up at the window. All I could see was a fist pounding behind the sofa cushion I'd jammed there. We needed a bigger couch. Privacy was important to my life-style. "Who *is* that?"

"Why don't you go up and see?" Chuck suggested.

"No way," I retorted. "We're taking down McKillPeople once and for all!"

"You wish," chortled the deep voice over the headset.

"The last time you tried that strategy," Pavel reminded me, "the fire department axed in your door."

The sensible advice came from Chuck. "It'll be a few minutes before we can get a new platoon together anyway. Go see who it is."

Bang, rattle! . . . "Cameron Boxer!"

"Just a minute!" I shouted.

Despite the clatter, I took my time going upstairs. After all, it wasn't like the entire Sycamore Fire Department was on my lawn—at least not this time.

I slipped out via the back slider and walked around the house to the front. The girl who stood pounding on the plywood was slight, almost compact, with medium-brown hair pulled back in a ponytail. Daphne Leibowitz. We'd been in school together since kindergarten, but I couldn't remember ever having a single conversation with her. Why was she suddenly standing on my porch, banging on the plywood and barking my name?

Spying me, she asked, "What happened to your door?"

"It's a long story," I replied, hoping that she wouldn't demand to hear it. Downstairs, Okinawa beckoned—and another shot at Evil McKillPeople, if he was still online.

"How do you get in and out?" she persisted.

"Around the back."

"Well, what are we waiting for?" she said impatiently. "We've got a lot of work to do."

I didn't like the sound of that—the *work* and the *we*, especially when they were used together. I doubted I'd said more than a few sentences to this girl in my entire life. There was no work, and there was definitely no *we*.

But Daphne didn't see it that way. She marched right past me, around the house, and in through the slider to the kitchen. Well, I couldn't very well leave her alone in there and go someplace else. And if I went back down to the basement, she'd just follow me.

"So, about this 'work' . . ." I said finally. The word burned my tongue.

"Good thinking. We should get to it." She opened her backpack, pulled out an iPad, and swiped the screen to bring up a web page.

I instantly recognized the logo of Sycamore Middle School. I leaned closer to investigate further.

> # POSITIVE ACTION GROUP
> ## "Because helping others is an education in itself."

I almost choked. That wasn't just *any* page from the school site. That was *my* page—and one of the illest ideas I'd ever had, too. My mother was so puffed up with pride over the Positive Action Group that her feet hadn't touched the ground in the three days since I'd first shown it to her. Dad was pretty psyched, too—at least, he hadn't mentioned the cost of the new door lately. And he'd taken to punching me playfully in the arm and calling me Mr. President. Even my kid sister, Melody, complained a little less about me hogging the game system. Nobody messed with a student leader, especially not with a class-A do-gooder like me.

Or so I assumed.

Daphne fixed me with earnest eyes. "Honest, Cam, this is the best thing ever!"

"I used to think so," I agreed miserably.

"Seriously, it restores my faith in the kids in this town. You must have changed a lot since that field trip where everything got canceled so we could search for you, and it turned out you were holed up in the bathroom playing video games on one of those handheld thingies."

I remembered that trip. The outdoor center. To be fair, it wasn't my fault nobody was smart enough to look in the bathroom. But I was glad they didn't. I reached level sixty-seven that day.

"So as soon as my membership goes through," she went on, "we can start planning our first big project."

"Membership?" I was mystified. "Membership in what?"

"The P.A.G., of course! I've got a ton of great ideas. There are so many people—and animals—who need help around here."

Maybe I was being extra clueless. But in my defense, it had never occurred to me that anyone would want to *join* the P.A.G. *I* wasn't even really a member, and I was the president. I would have bet a million dollars that nobody ever looked at the school site. And I would have lost, because one person did.

She was going on and on about some guy named Elvis. She talked really fast—or maybe it just seemed that way because I stopped listening after the first few sentences. I didn't even want *Daphne* in the P.A.G. If Elvis wanted to join, too, that would definitely put the membership way over the limit of zero, according to the club rules, which I was making up as fast as I could.

I had a flash of inspiration, and interrupted Daphne to say, "You know, the Positive Action Group is really new, and we're kind of worried about getting too big too fast. So right now there's a membership freeze. Sorry. But we'll let you know the minute that gets lifted."

Her tiny features flamed red and her ponytail seemed to defy gravity. "Sycamore school clubs have to be open to anybody. There can't be a membership freeze because that would go against every policy the district has. If you try to keep me out, I'll tell Mr. Fanshaw, Mrs. Amis, Dr. LaPierre, Ms. Katsakis, Mr. Del Zotto . . ."

She went on to list every adult with any authority over our lives, starting with the teachers, the principal, the superintendent, and Mayor Dolinka himself. I heard a couple of town council members in there, too, and maybe the chief of police. And all the while, I was thinking: *She'll do it, too. If I don't let her in, she'll rat me out to half of Sycamore, and before you know it, the P.A.G. will be exposed as a fraud. And when Mom and Dad find out, I can kiss Rule the World good-bye.*

What was I going to do?

"Okay," I said finally. "Join."

She brightened. "You mean I'm *in*?"

I nodded. "But I'm just making an exception for you. That Elvis guy is going to have to wait until the membership freeze is over."

She stared at me. "Elvis is a *beaver*!"

That made even less sense than the rest of it.

"Why would a beaver want to join the P.A.G.?" I asked.

"He's not a member; he's our first project. His colony got displaced when they built the new mall, but he was too old to keep up. We have to build him a new home."

"Don't beavers build their own homes?"

"Yeah . . . when they're in a colony. Poor Elvis is alone, and he's too old and feeble to build a whole lodge by himself. All he can do is chew on fences and decks and cable wires, getting yelled at by people who don't understand."

"Cable wires?" I repeated in horror. There had been a number of random cable outages around Sycamore lately, knocking out TV and Internet service, including my gaming connection. The cable company called the problems "unexplained," but those big beaver teeth were all the explanation I needed. Anybody who interfered with gaming networks didn't deserve a new home. He deserved a speedy exile.

"I've found the perfect spot for it," she raved on. "It's in the wooded part of Ravine Park, just north of the highway. There's a stream and plenty of sunlight coming through the treetops. Plus there are squirrels and chipmunks and all kinds of fellow rodents for him to make friends with so he won't feel so abandoned by his family."

It went without saying that the Positive Action Group

would never perform *any* good deeds, because I invented it purely to get my folks off my back. But even if the P.A.G. was 100 percent legit, the last thing it would waste its valuable time on was a beaver lodge. I had no idea what it *would* do, but beaver lodges would be last on the list.

But I couldn't very well tell her that, could I? So I said, "Okay, we'll bring it up at the next meeting."

"When?"

Daphne had a real knack for asking unanswerable questions. How could there be a *next* meeting when there had never been any meeting at all?

"I'll text you," I promised.

She made me write down her number. That paper was in the garbage before the sliding door had closed behind her.

CHAPTER FIVE
MR. FANSHAW

I hadn't been sleeping very well lately. The Fall Charity Raffle was on my mind. We'd only sold twenty-seven tickets, and I'd bought twelve of them. The drawing was less than two months away, and we didn't have anywhere near enough money to buy the prize—a 77-inch TV.

It was for charity. How could anybody not support charity? But these were middle school kids. Finding out what made them tick was like analyzing soil samples from the surface of Mars—a complete mystery. What they could do on their phones during the few minutes between classes would surpass any technology that existed when I was their age, but sometimes they had the maturity and attention span of newborn bats, sending out their first echo signals and then darting around following them in a pointless, directionless frenzy.

"They're kids," Dara Wemberley, our assistant principal, told me. "What do you expect from them? They're doing exactly what's appropriate at this age."

"Maybe," I replied sulkily. "But that's not selling any raffle tickets. I can't afford to buy them all on a guidance counselor's salary. And it's not going to look too kosher when *I* win the grand prize."

She just laughed and promised to buy another book of tickets. Maybe she was trying to help me out. Or, more likely, she figured the odds were in her favor because sales were slow. Who didn't want a 77-inch TV?

I sighed. It was all pretty understandable. These were tough times in Sycamore, with the new mall sucking the economic life out of the town. Families were regularly being asked to pony up for some campaign or other. We were running a book fair to support the library, the clubs and sports teams constantly had their hands out, and the PTA always had some fund-raiser going on. To ask these kids to spend what little spare time they had knocking on doors selling raffle tickets was probably going too far. I understood—I really did. But it wasn't going to look too good if the Salvation Army got stiffed and our school was still out the cost of one 77-inch TV.

I had to relax. Lack of sleep was making everything seem worse than it really was. A power nap would make all the difference in the world. Ten minutes was all I needed. I'd just lay my head down on the desk . . .

"Mr. Fanshaw?"

I snapped up again, the muscles in my neck protesting the sudden motion. Daphne Leibowitz leaned into my office. It would be unkind to say I wasn't glad to see her, but I'd almost been asleep, so I wasn't at my best. And Daphne was one of our regular customers in the guidance department. I wouldn't call her a fussbudget, exactly. She was a nice girl with a big heart. Seeing the world as it could have been was a wonderful quality in a young person. Expecting *me* to fix it for her—well, that wasn't in my job description.

"Hi, Daphne. What can I do for you?"

"I joined this new club," she began. "Don't get me wrong. It's really great and all that . . ."

"But?" I prompted. With Daphne, there was always a *but*.

"They're not doing anything!" she exclaimed. "The big planning meeting was supposed to be a week ago."

"Maybe you just had the wrong date and time," I suggested.

"There was no date and time. They were going to text me."

"Could they have forgotten?" I offered. It was a silly question. Nobody ever forgot Daphne. She had a knack for reminding people.

She shook her head. "I asked. There was no meeting. And there's no meeting scheduled yet. Honestly, Mr. Fanshaw, this club is the best thing, but they can't get it off the ground."

"I'll have a word with them," I promised. "Which club is it?"

"It's the P.A.G."

I drew a complete blank.

"The Positive Action Group," Daphne said. "I just know I can get them to help Elvis. Helping is the whole point of the group."

"Elvis?" I echoed. "Elvis died back in the seventies."

"Not the singer. The *beaver!*"

"Right. The beaver."

Let's just say that this was not the first time the beaver had come up in conversation with Daphne. I didn't realize the critter had a name. Elvis had eaten all the beautiful white bark off the base of the birch tree in my front yard. It hadn't brought the tree down, but it had weakened it enough to drop a big branch through the windshield of my car.

I swiveled toward my computer monitor. I knew every student club, team, group, and organization at Sycamore Middle. Why hadn't I heard of this Positive Action Group?

I browsed through the school's website. Sure enough, there it was.

POSITIVE ACTION GROUP

"Because helping others is an education in itself."

I was so bowled over that I just sat there, staring at the screen. How could an organization like this spring up right under my very nose? And such a wonderful organization, dedicated to helping people. Almost like the Friends of Fuzzy over at the high school, only not as aggressive. Some of those older teenage girls could be very pushy. To be honest, they scared me a little.

In my amazement, I completely forgot about Daphne, who was standing right across from me.

"Are you okay, Mr. Fanshaw? You just went all pale."

"Yes. Yes. I'm fine." And I was—*really* fine. Just the thought that someone had formed the Positive Action Group restored my faith in the youth of Sycamore.

I read the mission statement. Well, okay, it was a little short on specifics. No wonder they were having trouble getting it started. No problem. They needed guidance. That was where I came in.

"Thanks for bringing this to my attention," I told Daphne briskly. "Leave it with me. We'll have the P.A.G. shipshape in no time."

"And you'll tell them about Elvis?" she persisted.

I forced a smile. "You'll bring up the subject at the first meeting."

Satisfied with that, she left my office, and I returned to the website. After thirteen years as a guidance counselor, I knew enough not to get overly excited by the big plans of a bunch of middle school kids. Their hearts were in the right place, but their ambitions usually exceeded their capabilities. Still, I had a good feeling about the Positive Action Group. I was certain they were the kind of organization that would make a difference.

I read on:

MEET CAMERON BOXER, P.A.G. PRESIDENT

Cameron Boxer . . . *Cameron Boxer* . . . Why didn't I know that name? According to this, he was an eighth grader, which meant he'd been here more than two years. How could a community-minded student leader like this boy escape my notice for so long?

I called up his school record. The student card photo that appeared on my screen barely rang a bell. Light brown hair, blue eyes, pleasant-looking, but not memorable. I'd definitely seen him around, but never as anything more than a face in the crowd. In all the time he'd been here, I don't think he'd ever crossed my threshold. It seemed crazy that anyone could get so far along in his middle school career without ever once meeting the guidance counselor.

His grades were unremarkable—mostly low B's and the occasional C. And his extracurriculars . . .

I stared. There was nothing. I don't mean nothing special. I mean nothing at all. No clubs, no sports, no drama. If a student volunteered to hand out programs on Parents' Night, it would appear on this list. He didn't do that, either. The page was completely blank.

I examined the picture of the ambitious eighth grader who had created a group dedicated to community action. If I hadn't known better, I would've sworn that Cameron Boxer was a *slacker*.

It was just more proof that you couldn't judge a book by its cover.

I was anxious to meet with this fine young man and help him bring his blueprint for the Positive Action Group to fruition.

I could see it now. The P.A.G. was going to do a tremendous amount of good for the people of Sycamore.

And it seemed like the kind of organization that could sell a lot of raffle tickets.

CHAPTER SIX
CAMERON BOXER

"Can I take a bathroom break?"

I could always get out of Mrs. Herzlich's class that way. As I headed down the corridor, I was already scrolling through the apps on my phone. Bathroom break? Don't make me laugh. No self-respecting gamer ever needed a bathroom break. I was a camel. I once battled zombies for seven hours straight after drinking an entire half gallon of Gatorade. My back teeth were floating, but my mental discipline was 100 percent. I could have gone longer, too, if Evil McKillPeople hadn't ended my run early.

No, this was something different—a much-needed stress reliever in the middle of a long school day. There was no console here, obviously. But a little clan warfare could be waged right on your phone. It wouldn't count as practice for Rule the World. On the plus side, though, Evil McKillPeople wouldn't be able to muscle in. To be honest, I was starting to treasure the moments when I didn't have to worry about him crashing the party.

The upstairs boys' room seemed empty, but on second look, all the stalls were occupied. I wasn't going to let that stop me. I hadn't come for the atmosphere. I leaned up against a sink and tapped the app on my screen.

The game opened with the usual fanfare of horns. But as my well-fortified base appeared on my phone, I heard a second trumpeting—slightly muffled—from one of the stalls.

"Chuck?" I asked.

"No, it's me," came Pavel's voice from the center stall.

"I'm over here," Chuck added from the far end.

Another fanfare rang out—the final stall. The school could have saved a fortune on plumbing fixtures if they'd just put in a clan warfare room, but fat chance of that.

We hadn't been playing very long when there was a sharp rap at the door. Who knocked to get into the boys' room? How polite could a guy be?

"Sorry!" called Chuck. "All full up in here!"

And then a man's voice asked, "Is Cameron Boxer in there?"

I slid on my belly under a stall door, joining this kid Eric, who I didn't really know. He backed against the toilet tank and glared at me. I could relate. Gamers didn't like to have their space invaded—you know, unless they were playing Space Invaders.

"Why'd you have to come in here?" he rasped in complaint.

"You've got the handicapped stall," I hissed. "It has the most room."

There were footsteps in the bathroom. "Cameron Boxer?" the voice repeated.

I froze like a scared rabbit, intent on waiting this teacher out. Unfortunately, one of the other guys panicked and exited the game. This brought on another fanfare. The trumpets echoed off the tile walls as if heralding the arrival of some royal prince.

"Is that a cell phone?" the man asked suspiciously.

In answer, all three toilets flushed at the same time.

The voice was a little impatient now. "Cameron, is that you? Mrs. Herzlich told me I could find you here. I waited in the hall, but . . . Well, now I suppose I know why you were taking so long. Don't worry. Just this once, we'll forget about the cell phone."

Totally caught—curse you, Mrs. Herzlich—I slipped through the door, careful not to reveal Eric, cowering behind me, his feet on the toilet seat. To my surprise, the teacher wasn't a teacher at all. It was the guidance counselor, Mr. Fan-something. Fansteen, Fanboy—something like that.

Just to make it look good, I washed my hands. It was none of Mr. Fanbloom's business what I was doing in that stall.

He didn't seem mad that I was cutting class. As a matter of fact, he was smiling at me. That was almost scarier than the possibility of having my phone confiscated. It was bad enough that the guy knew my name, considering I hadn't done a single thing in more than two years to bring myself to his attention. The fact that he was happy to see me was *weird*.

"Well, Cameron, I have to tell you I'm impressed."

Correction: weird*er*.

"Our paths haven't crossed very often since you've been a student here," Mr. Fantasia went on, "so I suppose you can be excused for not knowing the rule."

"Rule?" Another word I wasn't super fond of.

"All new school clubs have to be approved by the guidance department."

So? What did that have to do with me? It was like he'd tracked me down to a bathroom stall to tell me the price of coconuts in Antarctica.

I had to come right out and ask, "Mr. Fan—uh, sir? What are we talking about?"

He gave me a conspiratorial look. "Daphne Leibowitz was in my office this morning. She's very excited about the Positive Action Group."

If he'd said I was about to be hung from the flagpole, I couldn't have been more shocked. The Positive Action Group? Nobody was supposed to know about that!

The minute Daphne showed up on the step in front of what used to be my door, I should have known. There was no way that bigmouth could keep quiet about the P.A.G.—not while that beaver was still on the loose.

But I couldn't mention any of that to Mr. Fandango.

"Uh—what exactly did Daphne say?" I ventured.

"Just how excited she is," the counselor replied. "She was anxiously awaiting your next meeting, and when it didn't happen, she became . . . frustrated."

Now the truth came out. It wasn't enough for Daphne to stalk me at my house and pull me away from my Rule the World training. She had to bring the guidance department down on my head. I'd kind of hoped to make it all the way through middle school without having to deal with guidance, because those guys could be murder on your lifestyle. But I guess my luck had just run out.

"And what did you tell her?" I managed, not really wanting to hear the answer.

"I told her there's nothing to worry about." He smiled even wider. "Every school club has to have a faculty adviser. I'm yours. So whatever questions you may have, I'm at your disposal."

He regarded me expectantly. That might have been the worst part. I didn't have any questions, and I definitely didn't want any answers.

When I said nothing, Mr. Fanta probed, "The first order of business should be to schedule a meeting, don't you think?"

I absolutely did *not* think. Still, I had to say something. "The problem," I began warily, "is that we're so *new* . . ."

He nodded understandingly. "Exactly how many members does the Positive Action Group have?"

Members? Exactly the same number as the Stick-Your-Head-in-the-Furnace Club and the Leap-the-Grand-Canyon Society.

"Well, there's me . . ." I fell silent and started counting on my fingers. To make it look good, I was going to have to include Pavel and Chuck—but I didn't want to get them trapped in this by saying their names out loud. I counted Borje, too. Mr. Fancy-pants didn't have to know he was in Sweden. He could be head of P.A.G. Europe. I threw in Evil McKillPeople, too, representing Canada, and also my sister, Melody, a sixth grader here. She wouldn't be too pleased about it, but with any luck, she'd never find out. Oh, and Daphne—the only person on the list who actually wanted to be there.

"Seven," I reported.

"That's a good core group," he approved. "There's a lot of work to do, though. We're going to need more members if we're going to make a dent in the needs of this community. Speaking of which, did you know that Sycamore Middle School is sponsoring a raffle to raise money for the Salvation Army? That's something the P.A.G. could latch onto and run with."

When I didn't say anything, he added, "Well, it's just an idea. We can worry about that later. The first order of business is recruiting. Why don't you see if Daphne can meet you in the art room after school to make some posters?"

There were times when you were playing a real battle game and you got pinned down, under fire, barely able to stay alive. That was how I had spent this whole face-to-face with Mr. Fantabulous—hunkered down, dodging bullets, trying not to get blown away. But in the game, sooner or later, your opponent would have to reload, or respawn, or even kill a spider walking up his wall. It was your chance to become *proactive*—to jump out of hiding and take the initiative with your own plan.

For the first time in this horrible conversation with Mr. Fanberg, a strategy opened up before me. The instant the final bell rang at three o'clock, I was going to be out of Sycamore Middle School so fast I'd leave a vapor trail behind me on the sidewalk. Daphne couldn't very well get mad at me for skipping out on a poster-making session she never knew existed.

Sure, it was sleazy, and I felt a little bad about the dishonesty. But not bad enough to put myself into the frying pan.

It was coming to me that all this was more than just a hiccup on the road to Rule the World. It was a direct threat to the lifestyle I'd spent more than thirteen years building up.

CHAPTER SEVEN
FREELAND MCBEAN

I got a D-minus on my essay on *To Kill a Mockingbird*. It didn't bother me. At least I didn't flunk, which wasn't bad considering I didn't read the book. How was I supposed to know Harper Lee wasn't one of the *Duck Dynasty* guys?

I got twelve out of sixty-seven on my math test, and I *did* flunk. It didn't bother me. Actually, I was amazed I got that many right.

I got a big fat zero on my social studies presentation because I didn't do one. It still didn't bother me. Mr. Silva held his extra-help sessions after school when I had football practice. First-String McBean didn't miss football for anything.

Then Coach called me into his office, and that *did* bother me. Because it wasn't to tell me about the highlight-film catch I made last week against Edison—one-handed, tiptoeing on the sideline, just in bounds.

It was to tell me I was off the team.

"String," he said—everybody called me String—"you're off the team."

It was like being blindsided by a linebacker—*if* there'd been a linebacker in our conference good enough to take down The String.

"But, Coach—*why?*"

"Academic ineligibility," he said sadly.

"Academic . . . ?"

"String, you haven't got the grades to stay on the team. Actually, you haven't got the grades to walk upright."

"What do *grades* have to do with football?"

"You know on our jerseys where it says 'Sycamore Middle School'? Well, the 'School' part is about grades. You don't pass, you don't play."

I was in agony. "Yeah, I know that, but—"

"But nothing," Coach told me flatly. "You're off the team until you start doing better in class."

"You can't do that to The String!" I protested. "It'll ruin my life. Or even worse, we'll *lose.*"

"I don't make the rules, kid. Improve your grades and we'll take you back."

Improve my grades—just like that! "Aw, how's *that* ever going to happen?"

"I might be able to work with you on that, Freeland," came another voice.

For the first time, I saw there was somebody else in the room. Coach always said, "When I'm talking, your eyes and ears are on me." That was probably why I never saw Mr. Fanshaw, the guidance guy, sitting in a chair in the corner of the office. How could I ever forget him? He was the only person in the whole school who didn't call me String. Maybe that was a guidance thing. They didn't do nicknames.

I was a drowning man thrashing for a life preserver. "Mr. Fanshaw, help me out here! I'm not a student—I'm a football player!"

"The thing is, Freeland, you have to be both."

Here it comes, I thought. The lecture on studying and working hard and becoming a well-rounded student athlete. The only rounded thing about me was my helmet. What Fanshaw and even Coach didn't understand was this: I didn't have *bad* work habits; I had *no* work habits. Or at least none that didn't involve catching, blocking, or running a tight pattern. If Fanshaw thought I was a dumb guy with Alvin Einstein trapped somewhere inside, then he was the dumb one.

Another thing Coach always said: In football and in life, the only important thing was results. It didn't matter what you said you could do, or what you had the potential to do. Just what you did.

So I was completely honest. "Mr. Fanshaw, I can't get good grades. I couldn't get them in kindergarten, and I can't get them now. I'm just not smart enough."

Coach got mad. "I don't want to hear that kind of talk. You can learn a playbook; you can read a defensive scheme. You're smart enough when it suits you."

Fanshaw made his pitch. "You only have to raise your grades a little bit. Nobody's asking for straight A's—that is, if you top it off with some really impressive extra credit."

I didn't know what that meant, but it sounded like hope. "Extra credit?"

His smile reminded me of the guy who'd sold Dad our last car. "Have you ever heard of the Positive Action Group?"

The story he told me lit a fire in my heart, which had been frozen solid by the idea of being shut out of football.

There was this club—the P.A.G. I forgot what they did, but it was definitely good, because Fanshaw was pretty amped about it. If I joined, and didn't totally bomb out in my classes, I could be back on the team in time for the playoffs.

"Where do I sign up?" I asked.

It was like a cloud had come to rain on Mr. Fanshaw's good mood.

"Well, the sign-up sheet isn't posted yet," he admitted, "because the posters aren't ready. I'm not sure what's taking so long. The boy who put it all together is obviously a visionary, but he's a little short on action. To be honest, he's hard to figure out. I think he might have an after-school job, because the minute school ends, he's gone with the wind . . ."

"Spit it out," Coach interrupted impatiently. "Is String going to be able to do this or not?"

"Of course. All he has to do is talk to Cameron." He turned to me. "Do you know Cameron Boxer?"

I did, and he didn't exactly strike me as the club-starting type. Cam was one of those gamer nerds. He hung out with that brainiac Pavel Dysan and that dweeb Chuck Kinsey. Chuck tried out for football back in seventh grade and broke three fingers in the first minute of the first practice. The team still did a modified version of his scream before every kickoff.

Did The String belong in a club with guys like that? Man, if it got me back on the Sycamore Seahawks, I would happily join the Church Ladies Knitting Team.

For some reason, Fanshaw was still hemming and hawing. ". . . and Daphne Leibowitz and I waited in the art room for two hours, but Cameron never showed . . ."

I said, "I'll talk to Cam."

"Really?" He seemed almost grateful, like I was offering him a lifeline, instead of the other way around. "Now, remember, you have to be firm with Cameron . . ." And off he went into another long speech about how hard it was to pin Cam down because his mind was working at such a high level.

"I'll pin him down," I promised. "When The String pins you, you stay pinned."

It wasn't that hard to find Cam. The String had connections. Ziggy, our QB, was dating this cheerleader, Shaleen. Well, her cousin's ex–lab partner in science, Dominic, was also in Cam's last class of the day, health. So I sprinted to the health room right at the bell—fastest time in the forty in county history. No one ran like The String.

Props to Cam—he was pretty fast, too. But I dashed past him and blocked the exit to the parking lot.

"I'm in," I told him.

He looked completely blank.

"The P.A.G., man!" I went on. "Fanshaw gave me the deets and I'm totally down."

"Great," he said. But he might as well have said *terrible*, because that's what it sounded like.

"Cam!" Chuck came running up, his backpack bouncing on his narrow shoulders. "We're still on after homework, right? I can't wait to—" He took one look at me and cradled his fingers protectively. "Hi, String."

"Is he in the club, too?" I asked Cam.

"What club?" Chuck blurted. "Wait—oh, *that* club."

"The thing is, uh, String." Cam was working really hard to choose the right words. "The P.A.G.—it's really complicated. I'm not sure we can put it together for this year."

I could feel my eyes narrowing. "We're eighth graders. What other year have we got?"

He was sweating now. "It takes time to iron out all the details. If we're going to do it, we have to do it right—"

"You're jerking The String!" I leaned into his face. "And The String doesn't like to be jerked. The P.A.G. is my ticket back onto the Seahawks. I need it. And when I need something, there's nothing more important than what I need."

I wasn't sure if Cam was getting my point, but I was definitely making an impression on Chuck. "You have to do it! He's The String!"

And then Cam Boxer did something that nobody else had ever done. He faked me out. He started to nod in agreement, ducked under my arm, and was out the door and gone, pounding through the parking lot toward the street.

Oh, sure, I could have run him down from behind. But I needed to get to the gym to stay in playing shape for when I rejoined the Seahawks later in the season.

There was no doubt in my mind that Cam would come through for me.

Nobody dared to let down The String.

CHAPTER EIGHT
CAMERON BOXER

I might have done too good a job selling my parents on the Positive Action Group, because now they hardly ever shut up about it.

"How come you never talk about how it's going?" my mother nagged. "We need details!"

My mom was breaking her arm patting herself on the back. She considered all this to be the result of tough love. She'd threatened to ban me from my lifestyle and I'd responded by becoming a student leader. It was probably the only time in her career as a mom where her strategic parenting had actually paid off.

"It's funny," my sister, Melody, put in. "Considering the Positive Action Group is such a big deal, nobody really knows about it. I haven't seen any notices or posters. There isn't even a sign-up sheet."

I glared at her. "There *is* a sign-up sheet."

"Where?" she challenged. "In the furnace room?"

"On the website," I gritted between clenched teeth. "You have to join online."

That part wasn't even a lie. Mr. Fanny-pack had insisted that there had to be a way for new members to come aboard. Luckily, Pavel had created a form where, as soon as you hit submit, you were redirected to a site based in Honduras where you could "buy" a square foot of the rain forest to protect it from developers. No matter how many times you went back, you still ended up in Honduras. It was pretty ill.

"Well, that makes sense," my dad concluded. "Everything's online these days. We have a website for the store. More and more people are doing their furniture shopping by computer."

He didn't look happy about it. A few online orders could never make up for all the customers lost to the new mall. Even the free-matching-love-seat promotion had been a bust. If I won Rule the World, I'd give the prize money to my parents to help with expenses until things improved.

If things ever improved.

Melody wouldn't let it go. She smelled a rat. "So who are some of your members?" she asked, the picture of wide-eyed innocence.

"Oh, you know. A bunch of people."

"Like who?" she persisted.

I threw it back in her face. "Freeland McBean, for one."

She looked impressed. "String? Really?"

"He practically begged me to let him join. Football stars like helping people, too, you know."

Her eyes narrowed. "The word around school is he's kicked off the team for not keeping his grades up."

I offered some big-brotherly advice: "You can't believe everything you hear in middle school, Melody." How come my sixth-grade sister was more tuned in to what was going on around school than I was after more than two years there? Wait—scratch that question. I already knew the answer. It was because she *cared*.

She didn't back down. "I still don't see how String found out about the P.A.G. in the first place when it's such a deep, dark secret."

"Maybe he heard from our *faculty adviser*," I retorted. "That's right, smart aleck. We have one, and you'll never guess who it is. Mr. Fan"—my mind went blank—"you know, the guidance counselor."

"That's enough," my mom said tiredly. She turned to Melody. "Your brother is finally involved in something worthwhile. Best of all, it has nothing to do with video games. The real question you should be asking yourself is why *you* aren't a member of the P.A.G."

"Because I can't afford sixty bucks for a square foot of rain forest!" Melody shot back.

She got in trouble for that—Mom thought she was sassing her. But it made me uneasy. That meant Melody had been on the web page, nosing around. And she could be like a bloodhound, especially when the target was me.

I called Pavel as soon I got back to my room. "My sister's onto us. We're going to have to do something about the online sign-up sheet."

He was amazed. "You want me to make it real?"

"Of course not. Just get it out of Honduras. If people end up at a different site every time they try to use it, maybe they'll think their computer's buggy."

He whistled. "And you thought your Melody problems were over when she started hanging out with that Katrina kid, leaving you the basement to yourself."

I sighed. "My Melody problems started the day they brought her home from the hospital. She barfed on my LeapPad and she's been a pain ever since. Now Mom wants her to join the P.A.G. Like that could ever happen."

There was silence on the line for a moment, followed by Pavel's voice, nervous now: "What if it *could* happen?"

"Come on, man. You know better than anybody that there's no such thing as the P.A.G."

"Maybe," he replied slowly. "But String McBean thinks he's a member, and what String thinks carries a lot of weight at our school."

I didn't like the sound of that. If Chuck had been the one worried, I wouldn't have given it another thought.

Chuck freaked out over report cards, Batman, talking to girls, and hurricanes forming off the coast of Africa.

But this was Pavel. Pavel was smart.

If he was worried, maybe there was something to be worried about.

CHAPTER NINE
JORDAN TOLEFFSEN

Felicia, my campaign manager, gave me the latest poll numbers, and the news wasn't good.

"You're losing to Kelly among sixth and seventh graders, and your eighth-grade lead is slipping."

"What? You said I was way out in front!"

"It was your debate performance," she said solemnly. "A lot of kids don't trust you."

I was appalled. "I'm the most trustworthy guy in the school!"

"You were sweating."

"It was a hundred and fifty degrees under those lights!"

"Kelly didn't sweat," Felicia pointed out. "Even Jordana didn't sweat, and she's only a seventh grader."

"Jordana!" I fumed. "Leave it to Kelly to drum up a third candidate with almost the exact same name as me. She knows half the kids won't be paying attention when they go to the ballot box. Jordan, Jordana—it's all the same to them. She's trying to siphon off my votes. The problem isn't the sweat; it's the *sleaze*."

She was patient. "You can stand here and complain that it's not fair, or you can do something about it. It's your choice, Jordan."

Felicia was like that—practical and sensible whenever I got too emotional. She was by far the best campaign manager in Sycamore Middle School. There was nothing she wouldn't do to help win an election. When I had that black eye from dodgeball, she put makeup on it so I wouldn't look like a punk at the all-candidates meeting for sixth-grade representative. In seventh grade, when I was accused of writing *STYROFOAM ROCKS* on the school's Earth Day bulletin board, she broke into the display case, dusted powder over everything, and revealed a handprint too large to be mine. By the time she got done spreading the word that I'd been unfairly accused, I came back from a twenty-point deficit and won a seat in the student senate.

But this was no grade-level election. This was for student body president.

I drew a deep breath. "Okay. What do I have to do?"

She began to tap on the laptop she used for official campaign business. "Kelly is a presidential scholar, so there's no way you're going to compete with her smarts-wise. She's also the captain of the girls' softball team, and let's face it, you couldn't catch a cold."

I was sarcastic. "Try not to build me up too much. You wouldn't want me to get a swelled head."

She took my arm and led me to one of my posters, taped to the wall.

There was a picture of me wearing a suit and tie—looking very presidential, if I do say so myself.

Felicia was all business. "What do you see? Or, more important, what *don't* you see?"

"You think we should put that Jordana Cohen isn't the same person as me and Kelly Hannity should be kicked out of the election for confusing voters?"

She regarded me pityingly. "Nobody votes for a crybaby."

"Not even if your opponent is being totally unfair?" I pleaded.

"Never use the phrase 'totally unfair.' It makes you sound like a crybaby. You can't turn this thing around by complaining about Kelly. You've got to build yourself up, focus on your own accomplishments."

I brightened. "Like student senate."

"That was last year. We have to show everybody who you are now. You need to get knee-deep in school activities."

I was mystified. "What could be more knee-deep than running for president?"

She pulled a paper from her pocket and unfolded it. It was the *Vote Kelly Hannity* flier that had been stuffed in every locker in the school. With a sinking heart, I took in the long list under *Extracurricular*: National Honor Society, Art Club, Athletic Leadership, Student Orientation Volunteers, Golf Team, Blood Drive Coordinator, Parents' Night Hostess . . .

It went on and on until I could barely stand it. This girl didn't have time to run for president. She didn't even have time to sleep. How could anybody ever compete with that?

"Looks like she's done it all," I mourned. "She hasn't left anything for anybody else."

"Not quite," Felicia countered. "I know one school organization she doesn't belong to."

"Yeah, right. If the undead formed a club, she'd find a way to get in to dominate the zombie vote."

"I'm serious," Felicia persisted. "It's called the Positive Action Group, and it's going to be huge."

I was unimpressed. "I never heard of it."

"It's new," she admitted. "That's probably why Kelly missed it. But I checked around. The faculty adviser is Fanshaw himself, so you know there's a lot of juice behind it. And you're going to be a founding member."

I was intrigued. "What do they do?"

She shrugged. "I don't really know, but the web page talks a lot about helping people. The main thing is you're in and Kelly isn't. And if she tries to join later, we can spread it around that she's copying you. It's a win-win."

For the first time, I saw a little light at the end of the tunnel. Politics went this way sometimes. You lose your lead because they bring in a seventh grader with the same name as you. But then you find a way to scratch and claw back to the top.

Okay, Felicia finds a way.

"So, did you sign me up?"

"I tried," she replied. "I think my computer's glitchy, because I kept getting sent to the wrong website. Anyway, this will be better. You'll join in person and make a public splash. The big mover and shaker is this guy Cameron Boxer. I know where his locker is."

A sour note sounded in my head. "Cameron Boxer? Are you sure? I know that kid. He's kind of a nobody. How important can this club be if he's in charge of it?"

"Big things start in small places," she lectured. "Abraham Lincoln grew up in a log cabin. Apple grew out of a garage. One day they'll say Jordan Toleffsen got his big break in the Positive Action Group."

Cam Boxer—I just couldn't imagine him being the founder of anything. Not if founding meant he had to get up off the couch.

We'd been neighbors our whole lives, but the only real interaction with him I could remember was the time we bought our dining room table from his family's store. He used to hang out on the big sectional sofas, playing on a handheld.

His locker was on the second floor—number 248B. Cam wasn't there, but Daphne Leibowitz was. She was taping a note to the metal door. I couldn't read what it said, but it had a lot of exclamation points.

As usual, Felicia broke the ice. "Have you seen Cameron Boxer?"

"Ha!" Daphne practically spat.

My campaign manager frowned. She had her phone out, ready to get a picture of my official entry into the Positive Action Group. This would be on the school's website by lunchtime and on the front page of the school paper tomorrow.

Daphne explained her comment. "Nobody sees Cameron Boxer. It's like seeing the wind. It can't be done."

I spoke up. "I'm joining the Positive Action Group."

"Yeah, good luck with that," Daphne said bitterly. "I've been trying to join for the past week and a half. Even Mr. Fanshaw's been stonewalled, and he's the faculty adviser. We need to schedule a meeting so we can get our first project going. Elvis has been eating out of the Dumpster by the train tracks. They found beaver droppings dangerously close to the electrified third rail. We have to create a habitat for him before he gets killed!"

Daphne talked really fast when she was angry. It was one of those tricky moments in politics. I had to have an opinion about this, but I really couldn't picture what the Positive Action Group or a dead singer had to do with beaver poop.

I said, "If I'm elected, I'll take care of that."

"What Jordan means," Felicia put in hurriedly, "is that he needs your vote for student body president. He wants to work with people like you and Cameron Boxer through the P.A.G. to make sure Elvis gets a fair deal."

"The only problem with that plan," Daphne complained, "is it has Cam in it. And nothing good can ever have him in it, even if it's something fantastic like the P.A.G."

I frowned. "So are you a member or not?"

Daphne shrugged helplessly. "Who knows? Mr. Fanshaw says I am, but how can I be? I can't pin down Cam, there's no sign-up sheet, and every time I go on the website, I end up in the rain forest."

"Well," Felicia persisted, "String's a member."

Daphne seemed surprised. "String McBean? How did he get in? Athletes always end up with special treatment."

"If he's in, you're in," Felicia concluded. She tapped her phone into camera mode. "Stand next to Jordan and I'll get a picture of you for the Sycamore *Middleman*."

While we were posing, an immense shadow loomed over us. "Where's Boxer?" rumbled a deep voice.

I looked up into the broad, leather-jacketed shoulders of Xavier Meggett. By sheer instinct, I backed away a step. I wasn't afraid of him—well, maybe just a little. Xavier was a tough piece of work, and two years older than the rest of us. He'd been held back a couple of times because his family sent him on these long "trips," which everybody knew meant he was doing another stretch in juvie. When you were running for president, you couldn't really hang around a kid like that; his bad reputation might rub off on you.

Felicia had the same idea. "Cam's not here." She was as anxious as I was to get rid of Xavier.

But he wasn't going anywhere. "So who's going to sign my sheet?"

I scanned the piece of paper he held out. It was a letter from Mr. Fanshaw addressed to someone whose position was identified as *Juvenile Probation Officer*. It explained that Xavier Pinkston Meggett would be completing his forty hours of court-mandated community service with the Positive Action Group. Attached was a time sheet, which had to be filled out and signed by a representative of the P.A.G.

"I guess you need Cam," I replied apologetically. "He's a little tricky to nail down."

I regretted those words as soon as they were out of my mouth. I hoped he wouldn't take the "nail down" part too literally and carry it out with real nails. This was Xavier, after all.

He heaved a sigh. "I was hoping to do this the easy way." Like there was also a hard way, and we really didn't want to know about it.

"Sorry," I told him. "But I can't put my name where it says Cam Boxer."

"It doesn't say Cam Boxer," Xavier observed mildly. "It says 'Authorized P.A.G. Representative.'"

Suddenly, Felicia snatched the paper from Xavier and shoved it under my nose. "Sign it!"

I was horrified. "But—"

"Now!" She took Xavier's pen and stuck it in my hand.

So I signed, and Felicia took a picture of me doing it, standing there beside this hulk who could cost me the election.

When we were on our way back downstairs, I turned on her. "Why did you make me do that? Now I'm forever going to be associated with that guy!"

"Don't you see?" she asked excitedly. "Not only are you a member of the P.A.G., you're an authorized representative! Second only to Cam himself!" She patted her phone smugly. "And I've got it all on camera."

The next day, when the *Middleman* came out, there was a picture of me right on the front page. I was signing the time sheet, but the photograph had been cropped so you couldn't even see Xavier.

The caption read: *Student government candidate and P.A.G. number-two man Jordan Toleffsen approves important court document for new group.*

I looked very presidential.

CHAPTER TEN
MR. FANSHAW

If I hadn't known better, I would've sworn that Cameron Boxer was trying to dynamite his own club. The P.A.G. had been in existence for more than two weeks, and still there had been zero activity.

I needed to talk to Cameron face-to-face. I sent an email to his school account. No response. I paged him over the PA system. He didn't come. Next time, I had the principal page him for me. No one ignored the principal.

No one except Cameron Boxer.

I tried to grab him after school, staking out his locker at the stroke of three. He never showed.

Freeland McBean noticed me there, waiting. "You're wasting your time, Mr. F. He's long gone."

I consulted my watch in dismay. "It isn't even three-oh-one yet! Not even the Flash could leave school so fast!"

I tried to catch up with him before school, but everyone assured me he wasn't a morning person. I was starting to think he had a black-market locker somewhere on the other side of the building. I had some detective work ahead of me.

I started dogging his classes. Considering I had his schedule and knew exactly where he was going to be, he was still hard to find. That boy spent more time in the bathroom than any fifteen students combined. He didn't need a guidance counselor; a doctor would be more to the point.

"Why is it so impossible to get in touch with Cameron Boxer!" I exclaimed in the faculty lounge.

It got a sympathetic laugh. As an eighth grader, he'd passed through most of the teachers' classrooms at some point.

"Stop by my room in seventh period," Barbara Lederer suggested kindly. "He's sure to be there."

I made a face. "The kid has a sixth sense. When he feels my aura approaching, he runs out to the bathroom."

"We're having our geometry unit test," she explained. "He has to be there or he flunks the course."

It worked. I waited patiently as Cameron finished his exam. Working away at his desk, he looked like everybody else, a normal young man. Was something wrong with me that I'd attributed Houdini-like powers to this ordinary boy? Had a trunk-load of unsold raffle tickets distorted my view of reality?

"All right, Cameron. I need to speak with you in my office."

"Sure," he agreed amiably. "I just need to hit the bathroom on the way."

"You can hit the bathroom *after* we talk." I wasn't born yesterday. "This won't take long."

Once in the office, I laid down the law. My philosophy had always been to let students take the lead, but you couldn't do that with Cameron Boxer. Actually, you couldn't do *anything* with Cameron Boxer, but especially not that.

I told him that the first meeting of the P.A.G. would be on Thursday in the music room, no ifs, ands, or buts. Sign-up sheets were going on all bulletin boards. It was a done deal, and the days of "we're so new" and "we're still getting our act together" were a thing of the past. Our act was officially together, and the P.A.G. was under way.

He seemed agreeable. Pleased, even. We shook on it.

By the next morning, all the sign-up sheets were gone, and so were the posters announcing the meeting.

"It has to be Cameron," I told Barbara. "The only things missing from the bulletin boards are the materials about the P.A.G. It was bad enough when he was ignoring his own club. Now he's actually working against it. The kid is driving me crazy!"

"Calm down," she soothed. "The boy started this group,

and now he's obviously having second thoughts. Shouldn't you find out why?"

She was right. I was a counselor. This kind of thing should have been up my alley.

So the next time I managed to corner Cameron, I put it to him just like that: "I think I understand what's bothering you. You're worried that if the P.A.G. isn't a success, everyone will blame you."

He just looked at me like I was speaking an ancient language that had been lost for six thousand years.

I took another stab at it. "Or maybe failure isn't the problem. Your concern is the extra responsibility of being president of such a high-profile organization."

He kept staring. It was honestly starting to freak me out a little.

So I said, "I promise you, Cameron, I've got your back on this. If you need a little leeway from your teachers, I'll speak to them. If you have trouble with any kids, you only have to come to me. I won't let anything go wrong."

What else could I do? Lie down and beg him to wipe his feet on me? I made myself his safety net. Whatever his reservations about the Positive Action Group, surely I had everything covered. I felt a rush of deep professional satisfaction. It was a shining moment for any guidance counselor, a rare chance to take a troubled student and insulate him from all the factors that were making him so conflicted.

He said, "Okay," and left the office.

I sat there, exhausted and not at all certain that Cameron Boxer would even show up for his own meeting on Thursday.

CHAPTER ELEVEN
CAMERON BOXER

It was perfect—until it wasn't perfect anymore.

"What are you going to do, Cam?" asked Pavel. "It's already Wednesday. That P.A.G. meeting is tomorrow after school."

"I guess I have to go," I said with resignation.

"And do what?" Chuck prompted.

I shrugged helplessly. "There *is* no P.A.G."

Pavel frowned. "I'm not so sure about that anymore. I mean, yeah, there *used* to be no P.A.G. But when there are posters all over the school, and the *Middleman* is writing about it, and Mr. Fanshaw's all gung ho, and people like Jordan and Xavier and String think they're members, it means there *is* a P.A.G. And *you're* the president of it."

I couldn't wrap my mind around that.

I wasn't even sure who to blame—Mr. Fantail, or Daphne, or String, or Jordan, or Xavier. Okay, not Xavier. It was never good for your health to blame Xavier for anything.

When the bell rang on meeting day, I marched through the halls like a prisoner on the way to his own execution. Without Pavel and Chuck at my side, I doubt I would have had the courage to put one foot in front of the other. We may have been the Awesome Threesome, but there was nothing awesome about what we were on our way to do.

Pavel and I hung back, but Chuck kept drifting ahead.

"What are *you* so enthused about?" Pavel asked him.

He flushed bright red. "I don't know. I've never joined anything before. I'm kind of excited to see what it's all about."

"You know what it's all about," I growled. "Nothing."

"Yeah, before," he conceded. "But now it looks like it's going to be about something. I'm anxious to find out what."

Chuck made more sense when he had a mouth full of gummy worms.

The door to the music room was open. Outside stood an easel with another one of Mr. Fanzine's signs:

P.A.G. MEETING TODAY
ALL WELCOME

That last part was a stab through the heart. *All Welcome* wasn't exactly the message I had in mind. *Danger: Toxic Waste* would have been more like it.

Inside, it was even worse than I thought it would be. Besides the guidance counselor and Daphne, String, Jordan,

Felicia, and Xavier, there were other people, too—kids who must have seen the posters and thought that *All Welcome* meant they could go. Some people would join anything just so they could add it to their résumé. And— my eyes must have bulged in horror—on the back row of risers sat Melody with her friend Katrina, both of them grinning at me. No way was this a show of sisterly support. Melody was here to drink in my misery—and enjoy every minute of it. She knew. You bet she knew.

Pavel and Chuck took seats in the far corner of the room, and I tried to make myself small between the two of them. No such luck. Mr. Fanblade hauled me up to the front of the room, his face glowing with purpose.

"Our president has arrived," he announced enthusiastically. "Let's get started. Take it away, Cameron."

So there I was, standing in front of everybody, with less than nothing to say and my sister in the back, taking notes. If I could do with myself what Pavel could do with websites, where he redirected people to other countries, I would have been in Iceland in a heartbeat.

The guidance counselor got sick of my dead silence and announced, "Why don't you tell us a little about what we have to look forward to in the Positive Action Group."

"Well, it's about helping, mostly . . ." I began, and then trailed off.

"And?"

"And assisting," I went on. I knew how stupid I sounded, but I was really cornered. "Aiding . . . You know, pitching in . . ."

My desperate gaze fell on my sister. No way was she going to bail me out. She hadn't had this much fun since watching me take the heat for the ziti. Pavel and Chuck had nothing to offer, either. Pavel regarded me in sympathy and Chuck seemed honestly interested in what I was going to say. Which was crazy, since he knew better than anyone that I had diddly-squat.

The rest of the kids were starting to get a little restless, because, let's face it, there wasn't too much information coming at them. All except String, who was leafing through a football playbook, and Xavier, who was asleep.

"Uh, doing our fair share . . . making Sycamore a better place . . ."

At last, my eyes fell on Daphne. She was leaning so far forward in her seat that she looked like she was about to tumble down the risers and land on her head. But seeing her there gave me my first flash of inspiration—a way to change the subject from the fact that I was laying a total egg at my own meeting.

"And most important of all," I blurted, "we've got to find a way to save that poor beaver out there!"

"Yes!!!" Daphne sprang to her feet. "We've got to create a home for Elvis! We're the Positive Action Group, and this is the most positive thing we could possibly do!"

She pounded the music stand in front of her, creating a gonging sound that woke up Xavier. He looked around, annoyed, and closed his eyes again.

"Elvis?" came a few confused voices. At least I wasn't the only person who'd never heard of him.

Daphne went into her emotional speech about the beaver who'd been uprooted by the new mall and abandoned by his colony and blah, blah, blah. I was more than happy to let her have the spotlight, so I sat back down between Pavel and Chuck. I wasn't a big Daphne fan, but once she had the floor, she was good for at least twenty minutes.

A few of the kids thought this was a great idea. Others weren't so sure. Shouldn't the mission of the P.A.G. be helping people, not animals? This went back and forth a couple of times, with Daphne's voice becoming louder and more shrill.

Then my darling sister put in her two cents. "Why are we arguing over this? We've got the founder of the P.A.G. right here. What do *you* think, Cam?"

What did I think? I wanted to be an only child, that's what I thought. Aloud, I said, "That gives us something to chew over until our next meeting."

"Next meeting?" Daphne wouldn't hear of it. "We're not done with *this* meeting!"

"Yeah, Cam," Chuck said earnestly. "We need to know *now*."

I stared at him in dismay.

Mr. Fanfiction bailed me out. "These are all really good questions. But as your faculty adviser, I've already set up the P.A.G.'s first project. The senior citizens' garden project on Seventh Street is due for its fall cleanup. I've volunteered us to help."

This announcement sucked all the energy out of the argument. The murmur that passed through the group was a little disappointed. But after all, who could complain about helping old people? Even Daphne, whose face was bright pink, bit her tongue and sat back down. One thing was definite: The way the guidance counselor had told it to us, it sure sounded like a done deal.

String looked up from his playbook. "Did I miss something?"

"We're going to be pulling weeds," Pavel supplied.

Xavier shifted to his left side and began to snore.

"I understand, people." The guidance counselor was smiling. "When you hear 'positive action' you picture yourselves saving the world, so gardening is kind of a letdown. But remember—every journey begins with the first step. This is real hands-on work, helping elderly people who might not be able to do it on their own. It's an excellent project to start with. Right, Cameron?"

"Sure." At that point, I would have said anything so long as nobody expected me to talk anymore.

Felicia rose, dragging Jordan with her. "The Toleffsen-for-president campaign is behind this one hundred percent." She reached around with her phone and snapped a selfie of the two of them to capture the moment.

One by one, the members of the Positive Action Group signed on to cleanup day at the senior citizens' garden project. Even Xavier opened his eyes long enough to nod.

"Mark your calendars," Mr. Faneuil Hall instructed the dispersing crowd. "Saturday, ten a.m. Don't be late. And keep selling those raffle tickets. Or, in the case of most of you, *start* selling them!"

Saturday, ten a.m. It was a slap in face. That was prime gaming time, especially if you were in training for Rule the World. But nobody cared about that.

"That was a pretty good meeting," Chuck commented as we exited the school. "And *you* were worried."

It said a lot for our friendship that I didn't even hit him.

CHAPTER TWELVE
DAPHNE LEIBOWITZ

Well, I wasn't happy. How could I be?

Not that helping the elderly with their garden wasn't a good thing. Of course it was! But winter was coming soon. All those senior citizens could go home to their warm houses and apartments, while Elvis would be left slapping his tail against cold concrete.

I didn't blame Mr. Fanshaw. He was just doing what he thought was best for the Positive Action Group. It was Cam Boxer I was mad at. As P.A.G. president, it was his job to make sure we tackled important problems. Digging up dead plants and yanking out weeds hardly counted as that. He knew the misfortunes and dangers Elvis faced every single day—I'd told him myself that time I went over to his house. I should have known better than to expect leadership from a guy with a sheet of plywood for a front door!

At the meeting, I was so devastated that I almost quit on the spot. But who would speak up for Elvis if I wasn't even a member? After all, Mr. Fanshaw didn't say we could *never* build a beaver habitat, just that it wouldn't be first.

No, I had to stick with the Positive Action Group.

I would go along with all their plans, doing everything they did, only better. I'd be the greatest garden-helper those senior citizens had ever seen. I intended to make myself indispensable to the P.A.G. And when it got to the point that they couldn't function without me, I'd demand that they do something for Elvis.

I arrived at the seniors' garden early on Saturday. Wouldn't you know it? Everybody else was late. It was the first cold morning of the fall. There I stood, fuming and shivering. An icy drizzle began to come down.

I decided to start working right away. That way, Mr. Fanshaw would see how motivated I was. And a little physical activity might warm me up. One problem: I wasn't much of a gardener, so I wasn't sure exactly what to do.

Weeding would definitely be a part of it. That was as good a place to start as any. I surveyed the patchwork of garden plots that stretched clear across the lot. There was definitely no shortage of weeds.

I bent over a long stringy stalk and pulled. It wouldn't budge. I tried again, grabbing on with both hands and putting some back into it. Nothing. So I braced my legs, angled my back, and heaved with all my might. I staggered back a few steps as the weed popped out. And there, dangling at the end of it—

"Hey—what do you think you're doing, pulling up my prize turnips?" came an angry voice behind me.

A little old lady who probably didn't come up as high as my shoulder stalked toward me, gesturing angrily with a garden claw. She was dressed in so many layers of sweaters, vests, and coats that she waddled. But she still managed to make her approach look menacing.

"Those are my turnips! I leave them in until the snow flies so they're perfect for Thanksgiving!"

"Sorry." I dropped to my knees and tried to stuff the big, rock-hard vegetable into the crater I'd opened up in the ground. It didn't fit.

"Too late now. You can't transplant a mature turnip. Everybody knows that. It's *ruined*." Her eyes shot sparks. "What are you doing here? This is private property."

Actually, it was public property, but I didn't tell her that. She was still wielding that claw, and I didn't have a weapon, except maybe the turnip—which, come to think of it, probably could have taken out a charging rhino.

It must have looked like a fight was brewing, because when Mr. Fanshaw showed up, he ran between the two of us like a referee breaking up a boxing match.

"Hello there!" he said breathlessly. "We're the Positive Action Group from the middle school. We're here to help."

"It's my fault," I admitted. "I thought this turnip was a weed and I pulled it out."

"Never you mind, dear." The claw lady did a complete about-face. I was no longer a turnip murderer. I was a doer of good deeds.

As it turned out, the senior gardeners were really grateful to have some help with their fall cleanup. As one after another came out to thank us, I felt a little guilty that I'd been so against this idea. It was my loyalty to Elvis, of course. But some of the seniors were in their nineties and a couple might have been over a hundred. The manual labor of bending and weeding and digging would have been too much for them.

Mr. Fanshaw had brought Xavier and String with him. He probably figured that the only way those two would show up was if he drove them personally. I was interested to see if our club president would bother to put in an appearance. But to my surprise, everybody came—all fourteen P.A.G. members, including Cam.

Each volunteer was assigned to a senior gardener who would supervise the work. I got Mrs. Demarest, the claw lady, who loved me now. And with her telling me the difference between the weeds and the turnips, I was doing great—especially since *I* had the claw.

I wasn't so sure about the others, though, especially Xavier. He'd been paired with this cranky old guy, who was bossing him around, never satisfied with anything

Xavier did. It was all "No, that's not right!" and "Don't do it like that!" and "What did I just tell you?"

I was getting a little nervous, and so was Mr. Fanshaw, because Xavier was, well, *Xavier*. He wasn't known for his patience and gentleness. And if he lost it with Mr. Meanie, it wasn't going to reflect well on the P.A.G., no matter how much the nasty geezer had brought it on himself.

"Oh, yeah! Look at that dirt fly! Nobody digs like The String! Can you dig how I'm digging?"

Another problem: That jock, that showboat, String McBean, had to treat everything like it was a competition. There he stood in a blizzard of topsoil, his shovel just a blur, bombarding silver-haired ladies with earth, trash-talking some imaginary opponent. "Don't even bother trying to keep up, losers. It can't be done."

Not everybody was as annoying as String. Most of us worked hard and did an okay job. But there was plenty of goofing off as well, and a lot of mud balls aimed at the backs of heads. Cam and that Pavel kid were kind of dogging it, but their friend Chuck was hoeing, and seemed to be taking this at least semiseriously.

When I looked over to see how Mr. Fanshaw felt about how things were going, I noticed that we had company. A short, squat woman stood talking with the P.A.G. faculty adviser. She huddled under an enormous umbrella, even though it was hardly raining anymore. It wasn't until I spotted the notebook in her hand that I recognized her from her byline photo in the newspaper. It was Audra Klincker, who had a weekly column about happenings around town in the Sycamore *Gazette*.

If she was here to write an article about the P.A.G., it would be amazing PR, and a lot more kids would want to join up! I tried to read her expression to see if she was impressed. But at that moment, she turned away to watch String, who had spiked his shovel and was performing his touchdown dance on somebody's rhubarb plants.

That was when I noticed a familiar slapping sound. I wheeled around.

I gawked. I goggled.

About ten feet behind String was a large brown bundle of fur. Beady black eyes watched the touchdown dance while a flat tail whacked at a mud puddle. A half-eaten plum tomato stuck out from behind buckteeth.

Elvis!

I was just about to cry out when an angry voice exclaimed, "Get away from my tomatoes, you mangy rodent!"

Before I knew it, one of the senior citizens was running after Elvis, waving a long-handled rake over his head!

"Sir!" Mr. Fanshaw called in alarm. "Please be more careful with that around the children!"

But the man continued to chase the poor beaver, and

for an old guy, he could really move. He was definitely one of the youngest of the seniors, probably in his sixties. Not that I cared about that. If he was a danger to Elvis, it didn't matter to me if he was a hundred and fifty or three and a half.

Thunk! He swung the big rake. The tines bit into the earth just a few inches behind the beaver's wide, flat tail. Elvis hustled away at his top speed, which wasn't very fast at all.

That did it. Everybody started yelling at the same time, seniors and kids alike. To my horror, a lot of the gardeners were cheering for the guy with the rake. I guess the tomato wasn't the only vegetable Elvis had stolen from this garden. But being hungry shouldn't be the kind of crime you paid for with your *life*!

There was no time to make up my mind. I acted on pure emotion. That animal abuser had to be stopped, and there was only one way to do it. I threw myself at his legs, clamping my arms around his knees. He went down like a sack of potatoes, with a loud *"oof"* as the two of us hit the ground. I face-planted in the dirt, which wasn't fun. But I was rewarded by the sight of Elvis making his getaway.

The fallen gardener scrambled up and turned blazing eyes on me. "Is that your idea of *helping*?"

The last person I ever would have expected to come to my defense hauled me to my feet and stood in front of me. String.

"That's not it!" the football star exclaimed reverently. "It was a tackle—a highlight-film tackle! The String couldn't have done it any better himself!"

The old guy was spitting mud. "And that makes it okay? I've got arthritis in those knees!"

Mr. Fanshaw rushed over to him. "Sir—we're so sorry—"

"I'm not!" I interrupted. "He was trying to kill Elvis!"

"That thieving woodchuck has been helping himself to our vegetables all season!" the man charged.

"He's not a woodchuck—he's a beaver! And we should all have sympathy for a poor soul kicked out of his colony and left behind to starve. Is it too much for you to sacrifice one lousy tomato to make his life more bearable?"

"I'd be thrilled to give him a tomato," the man insisted. "But he won't eat *one* tomato—he takes a bite out of all of them. And the peppers, too. And the cucumbers."

I was about to snap back at him—but then I noticed Audra Klincker. She was huddled beneath her giant umbrella, jotting notes at a furious pace, a disapproving look on her face. And I thought: As much as this old stinker deserved to be screamed at, it wouldn't look good if this week's Klincker Kronicle was about how a member of the Positive Action Group did a negative action like tackling one of the senior citizens she was supposed to be helping.

Even if it was a highlight-film tackle.

CHAPTER THIRTEEN
CAMERON BOXER

Who knew that being a good person would turn out to be so boring? Seriously, I gave up an entire day of video games for *this*?

"Boring?" Pavel laughed at me. "Haven't you been paying attention? Daphne *tackled* a senior citizen. It's the first time I've ever seen String compliment someone other than himself."

"Yeah, real entertaining," I muttered. "I thought that reporter lady would have a heart attack when Daphne laid that guy out. If my parents read in the paper that the P.A.G.'s bad, I'll be right back where I started—no Rule the World."

"Forget Daphne," he told me. "Worry about a real problem. That cranky guy who's bossing Xavier around doesn't realize he's juggling nitro. If he wakes up across town, that won't just be in the Klincker Kronicle. It'll make the front page."

"I need a break," I complained.

"From what?" Pavel challenged. "Technically, you haven't moved a single molecule of earth. Look at Chuck. He's weeded two whole plots already."

It was true. For some reason, Chuck was treating today like it was a real thing. Old ladies were lining up to get his attention. He was the darling of the senior citizens' garden. Where would a member of the Awesome Threesome get such a bad attitude?

"Well, I'm the president," I grumbled, "and I still say that the Positive Action Group doesn't exist."

"I hate to break it to you," Pavel retorted, "but it's existing all around you in living color. There's even a reporter here to record it for posterity."

I sighed. "Mr. Fanorama's busy trying to calm down the tackled guy. I'm going to check my clan."

"Your phone will get wet."

"I'll sneak into the lobby of the apartment building next door. Cover for me."

"But . . ."

I left him standing there. If I didn't get something decent into this wasted day, I was going to lose my mind. Besides, the way clan warfare worked, you could actually be invaded while you were offline. I didn't have that much faith in my fellow clan members to ride to the rescue and defend my base for me.

Anyway, I'd cover for Pavel later so he could check on his own clan—and for Chuck, too, if he could tear himself away from all that helping.

With the guidance counselor distracted, it was easy to

complete my disappearing act. I ducked in the side entrance and stood in the stairwell as the app opened with its usual fanfare.

Sure enough, I'd suffered two attacks, although the damage wasn't serious. As I made the necessary repairs, I couldn't help noticing a puddle of water forming at my feet. At first I assumed that rain was leaking in from outside. Then I noticed a tiny trickle running down the steps. Curious, I followed it up to the second floor. It was traveling in a thin stream, shining in the fluorescent lights.

The game app chirped an alert. I ignored it. That didn't really go with my lifestyle, but by this time, I was really interested to see where the water was coming from. I traced the trickle to the door of apartment 206. There, it was more than a trickle. It was burbling out over the door saddle.

I knocked. "Hello? Uh—I think there's a leak in your apartment." I heard a faint voice, and a shuffling sound. Someone was definitely in there, but nobody came.

The game chirped again, and I was sorely tempted to go back to it. After all, this was none of my business. And whoever was in 206 obviously didn't need my help, or he would have answered the door.

Maybe.

I thought of another situation where a guy didn't respond

to the people who were trying to tell him something bad was happening to his house. That guy hadn't answered the door, either—and now he didn't have one, because the fire department had smashed it up. I seriously doubted that anyone in a senior citizens building was ignoring my knock because he was battling Evil McKillPeople. But it seemed like somebody in there was in trouble.

I called Pavel, but he didn't pick up. Chuck didn't answer, either. It figured—the guy was so occupied with his fan club of old ladies that when he was needed for *real* helping, he was AWOL.

Out of options, I ran back downstairs, my sneakers splashing in the growing stream. I burst out of the building, waving my arms and yelling. Everybody was going to know that I'd been goofing off, but I couldn't worry about that now.

"Come quick!" I bellowed. "There's an emergency!"

Mr. Fanatic shot me an angry look. "Cameron, what do you think you're doing?"

String must have been tired of showing off, because he dropped his shovel and started toward me. "Let's go! Our president needs us!"

I doubt anybody there cared that I was president, but by this time, the volunteers were anxious for a break. They all came running, even Xavier, who seemed relieved to abandon his obnoxious taskmaster.

"Where's everybody going?" our faculty adviser demanded.

Scowling beside him, Audra Klincker was making notes again.

My loving sister, Melody, came roaring up to me, Katrina hot on her heels. "What's going on, Cam? What are you up to now?"

"Why do you assume it's a bad thing?" I demanded.

"Because I know you!"

There was no time to fight with her. I led the troops up the wet steps and down the hall to 206. We left a trail of mud behind us, earth from the garden mixing with the steady trickle from upstairs.

"That's where the water's coming from!" I explained breathlessly. "There's someone in there, but nobody answers!"

"Stand back!" ordered Freeland McBean. "No door is a match for The String!" He hurled himself at 206, bounced off and landed in a heap on the floor.

It was the first time I ever saw Xavier smile. The big guy pulled a fire extinguisher off the wall and delivered a heavy blow to the doorknob. There was a crack and the door swung open.

Mr. Fantasy pounded to the top of the stairs just in time to witness this. "Aw, Xavier!" he moaned. "You promised you'd stay out of trouble!"

We burst into the apartment, and that's where we saw the elderly woman who lived there. She had begun to fill the kitchen sink to do her dishes, tripped, and hit her head on the marble counter. She lay on the tiles, semiconscious, the overflowing water puddling around her and streaming past her, down the hall, and out the front door.

We could hear Audra Klincker's shrill voice all the way down the hall. "This isn't a Positive Action Group; it's a wrecking crew! I'm calling the police!" She burst to the front, her cell phone at her ear, and froze at the sight of Xavier helping the victim sit up and lean against him. Pavel rushed to turn off the tap.

Xavier looked at the reporter. "An ambulance would be better."

CHAPTER FOURTEEN
MELODY BOXER

It went without saying that my brother was an idiot. It was bad enough sharing a house with him when there was a working front door and you could make a quick getaway. But *our* house . . .

Sigh.

If I had to listen to one more lecture about Cam and his "lifestyle," I was going to lose it. Cam's so-called lifestyle was just an excuse to be a video-game-addicted couch potato.

I longed for Mom and Dad to see through Cam's smoke screen. I *prayed* for it. I thought it had finally come the day of the scorched ziti. I was *so* happy.

But no. Suddenly, there was the P.A.G., and Cam was off the hook again.

So imagine my reaction when I saw the front page of the Sycamore *Gazette*.

The Klincker Kronicle

POSITIVE ACTION TURNS TO HEROISM FOR MIDDLE SCHOOLERS

By Audra Klincker, *Gazette* Staff Reporter

It's a scenario all parents are familiar with. Youngsters "helping." We applaud their noble goals, but, intentionally or not, they often do as much harm as good.

These thoughts were uppermost in my mind as I trekked out to the senior citizens' garden project on Seventh Street to observe the first good deed of the Positive Action Group, a new community service club at Sycamore Middle School.

What I saw there at first was exactly what I expected to see—well-meaning tweens and young teens, some of them working, some of them a little rowdy. If their hearts were in the right place, their gardening skills left something to be desired. Many didn't know the difference between a weed and a vegetable. The kids might have shown a little more sensitivity toward their elderly hosts.

Then true heroism emerged. A small trickle of water in the building next door caught the attention of Cameron Boxer, the P.A.G. president. His quick thinking led to the rescue of Mrs. Isadora Klebner, 78, after a household accident. Every single member of the P.A.G. contributed wholeheartedly to this errand of mercy. All citizens of Sycamore owe them a debt of gratitude and a hearty "well done."

Most impressive of all is Cameron Boxer himself, a modest young man who never toots his own horn and always steps back from the spotlight. "Please don't write about this in the Gazette," he begged me, after the ambulance had taken Mrs. Klebner away to a hospital. I honestly got the impression that he would have been happiest if I had forgotten the whole thing.

Well, tough luck, Cameron Boxer. You and the boys and girls of the P.A.G. are heroes in Sycamore today.

I honestly wanted to rip out the article with my teeth, chew it up, spit it out, and flush it down the toilet. Bad enough my brother conjured up a fake club to fool Mom and Dad into believing he'd changed his slacker ways. But now he was a hero for it?

I'd always known that Audra Klincker was a crummy journalist, and here was the proof. Nobody bothered to ask what Cam was doing in that apartment building to begin with. I could have told them. It was because their "hero" couldn't go more than forty-five minutes without video games. For sure he was playing on his phone when he noticed that trickle of water. The amazing thing was that he *did* something about it. Normally, Cam wouldn't pause a video game if his house was on fire. Oh, yeah—it *was*. And he *didn't*. And we had the "door" to show for it.

Sigh.

Don't get me wrong. I liked video games, too. But Cam was such a console hog that I had to go over to Katrina's if I wanted to play. I tried to get him to draw up a schedule so we could share the system. You know what he said? That I wasn't a "serious gamer on an ill level" like him. And Mom and Dad were too preoccupied with the store to realize how unfair their darling son was being.

Speaking of my parents, they were ecstatic over Audra Klincker's article. Face it, she had painted a picture of the son they'd always wanted to have. Pretty soon the clipping held the place of honor on our refrigerator, right above the latest circular for Boxer's Furniture Showroom.

Well, I knew exactly why my flake brother had started the Positive Action Group. And it had nothing to do with helping senior citizens, or anybody else.

My mother was annoyed with me. "You're just jealous, and there's no reason for it. You're a P.A.G. member, too. This article is also about you."

"Yeah," I agreed without enthusiasm. "I'm 'every single member.' I better hire a bodyguard to fight off the paparazzi." I'd only joined the P.A.G. so I'd have a front-row seat when my brother's creation blew up in his face. The last thing I expected was for Audra Klincker to turn him into a knight in shining armor.

I added, "You know why Cam was in that apartment building in the first place? He was gaming while we were all working. Doesn't that sound a little bit more like him than 'hero'?"

No matter what I said, what argument I made, my parents refused to see it. I was just the resentful little sister jealous of all the attention my brother was getting.

Was I jealous? Why wouldn't I be? If I pulled something like this, I'd be swatted down like a gnat. Just watching Cam getting away with it was giving me cramps.

"You're so lucky to be an only child," I told Katrina as I slumped into the beanbag chair in her room, surrounded by her posters of Star Trek, Star Wars, and Battlestar Galactica. I needed to relax with some video games.

I reached for the controller and froze. "Wait a minute. What's that doing there?"

Taped to the wall, obscuring Jabba the Hutt, was today's Klincker Kronicle.

"Didn't you see it?" Katrina asked.

"See it? My parents bought twenty copies! Why do *you* have it?"

She looked surprised. "Didn't you have fun on Saturday?"

I made a face. "I'm still trying to get the mud out from under my fingernails."

"It was *amazing*!" she exclaimed. "Sixth graders are total nobodies in middle school. But in the P.A.G., you hang out with upperclassmen. You know String McBean actually smiled at me? And my best friend's brother is the head of the whole thing!"

I just stared at her. How could two people live through the same experience and see it so differently?

"And the part where we saved that lady's life, obviously," she added. "That was pretty cool, too. Cam was awesome! Does he have a girlfriend?"

Sigh.

First my parents, now Katrina. Was there no escaping my stupid brother?

CHAPTER FIFTEEN
CAMERON BOXER

Things were changing, and I didn't like change.

When I walked down the hall, people I didn't know said hi to me. Some of them wanted to stop and talk about the Positive Action Group and the heroic thing I did last Saturday when that lady almost drowned herself in her own kitchen. Worse, they all wanted to join the P.A.G. And even if they didn't, their parents wanted them to. The sign-up sheets were full of names, and Mr. Fanbelt said we had to have another meeting to decide on our next project. And this time we couldn't use the music room because we had too many members. We had to find a place that could fit everybody.

I got called to the office to be congratulated by the principal, and the assistant principal, and the other assistant principal, and the other other assistant principal.

Dr. LaPierre wondered how it could be that he'd never met me before, and I was tempted to say: *That was no accident. That was part of a very careful plan.*

Well, that plan was falling apart with every passing hour, thanks to the Positive Action Group. Everybody knew me now—students, teachers, administrators. Even the lunch ladies were loading up my tray with extra broccoli and mashed potatoes. I'd worked so hard to create a bubble around myself, letting in only the people and things that really mattered. That bubble was totally gone.

"We should have seen it coming," Pavel told me as we stopped at my secret locker—the one I used so the teachers wouldn't know where to find me. "Technically, there was always a chance that the P.A.G. would catch on."

"It's Mrs. Klebner's fault," I complained. "Why couldn't she have been more careful?"

"What's so bad about the Positive Action Group?" asked Chuck. "It turned out to be a lot of fun."

I opened the locker, and the smell nearly knocked the three of us over. Perfume—strong, sickly sweet, and floral.

"Dude!" Pavel exclaimed. "Don't you ever air out your gym shoes?"

"That's not it," Chuck said breathlessly. "Look." There, atop the pile of sweaty socks and old T-shirts, sat a folded piece of pink stationery. "Someone must have slipped it in through the vent in the door."

I picked it up delicately, between thumb and forefinger. That's where the stink was coming from, all right. I headed for the trash can.

"Don't you want to see what it says?" asked Chuck.

I shook my head. "It reeks. That's all I need to know."

"You have to find out who it's from," Pavel reasoned. "Whoever it is knows about your secret locker."

The instant I unfolded the page, the smell tripled.

Dear Cam,

I want to tell you that what you did was just amazing! Everybody says you're a hero, but I know you're much more than that. You're a superhero—even though you don't have special powers or whatever . . .

"Ooooh!" trilled Chuck. "Cam has a girlfriend!"

"Romance is in the air!" added Pavel, his nose wrinkled.

My gaze skipped down the page. All the *i*'s were dotted with little hearts, and there was a red lipstick impression of a kiss in the bottom corner. It finished:

Your fellow pagger,
Katrina Bundy

I felt my ears burning. Bad enough to have a secret admirer, but why did it have to be my sixth-grade kid sister's sixth-grade kid friend?

No wonder she'd found this locker. Melody must have told her about it.

Chuck read over my shoulder. "What's a pagger?"

"I think she means P.A.G.-er," Pavel mused. "It's kind of catchy, actually."

"It's the stupidest thing I've ever heard in my life," I said sourly.

"Not really," Pavel reasoned. "She has a crush on you, so she's calling attention to the things you have in common. You're a couple of paggers."

"What could be sweeter than two young paggers in love?" Chuck chimed in.

I tore the note into confetti and threw it in the trash. "If you morons want to *not* be my partner for Rule the World, then keep up the good work. I'm leaving."

I slung my backpack over my shoulder and stormed out on them.

I calmed down a little on the walk home. It was the first time all day that I'd taken three steps without hearing my name coming from some unfamiliar mouth.

That was when I noticed a bright red Dodge Charger driving very slowly, matching my pace. The passenger window rolled down and the driver leaned across the empty seat. "Cameron Boxer?"

It was a question, which was a good sign. It meant he didn't know for sure. I stuffed my hands in my pockets and kept going, eyes straight ahead.

With a squeal of tires, the Charger lurched past me, then bumped up onto the curb to cut me off. The back door was thrown open.

"Get in the car!" barked a girl's voice.

I backed away and peered inside. There sat the most drop-dead-gorgeous girl I'd ever seen. She had long dark hair and green cat's eyes that glowed like the emeralds in Bejeweled. She wore a cheerleader's outfit: short skirt, tight top, black boots with silver tassels. Two massive pom-poms lay on the seat.

I knew her. Everybody did. She was Jennifer Del Rio, a senior at Sycamore High—head cheerleader, home-coming queen, and this year's Grand Pal of the Friends of Fuzzy.

"Get in!" she insisted. And when I took the seat beside her, she reached around me and slammed the door shut. "Drive, Tony."

We peeled away, thumping off the curb. The car's locks ominously snapped shut.

She fixed me with her Bejeweled stare and slammed a newspaper clipping between us. "Explain this."

It was Audra Klincker's article.

"Well," I explained, "we were helping with the senior citizens' garden project, and I noticed something in the apartment building next door—"

"Do you think I waste one sleepless second stressing

over what some middle schooler noticed in an apartment building?" she demanded.

"It was a trickle of water," I supplied.

"I don't care if it was dragon's blood! What is this Positive Action Group, and where do you get off doing community service on *my* turf?"

"*Your* turf?" I echoed.

"The good deeds around here are done by the Friends of Fuzzy. You know that. Everyone knows that."

"That's the way it is," added Tony, scowling at me in the rearview mirror.

I was bewildered. "Can't we all do good deeds? They're—you know—*good.*"

Jennifer Del Rio wasn't nearly as attractive when her face twisted in fury, her full lips disappearing into a thin line. "Pretty soon my college application is going in to Harvard, and I'm going to throw the kitchen sink at them. Every piece of civic service, or charity, or good citizenship that could possibly happen in a one-horse town like Sycamore is going to be on there. I'd love to put that I helped the senior citizens clean up their garden. But I can't—*because a bunch of snot-nosed middle schoolers beat me to it!*"

Tony turned around, peering over the seat and completely ignoring the road ahead. "That wasn't very nice of you," he admonished.

"I'm on your side," I told Jennifer. And it was the truth. "The P.A.G. is a pain in my butt."

"So what's the problem?" she demanded.

"Mr. Fan—uh—the guidance counselor," I explained. "He loves the P.A.G. If it was up to me, I'd drop it in a heartbeat."

Jennifer refolded her long legs, the tassels on her boots sparkling. "See to it that it *is* up to you." She peered out the window. "This is your stop."

I followed her gaze. We were in the middle of nowhere, outside the town limits, driving along a two-lane rural road. "No, it isn't."

Tony pulled over to the shoulder. "Jennifer says this is your stop. So this is your stop." The locks clicked open.

"But my house is really far from here."

The head cheerleader opened the door for me. "I like a nice walk. It's a great chance to think about what's really important in life."

It took me forty-five minutes to get home.

CHAPTER SIXTEEN
MR. FANSHAW

When Audra Klincker telephoned to ask about the Positive Action Group's next move, I was excited to talk it over with the P.A.G. president.

But when I mentioned it to Cameron, he seemed reluctant, even alarmed. "So soon?"

"Why not? The garden project was a hit." I chuckled. "We can't expect to save a life every time, but we're on a roll. We have five times the members we had before. We can tackle something even more ambitious!"

He turned positively green and started sputtering about not rushing into things. I swear, if I could figure this kid out, I'd win the guidance counselor equivalent of a Nobel Prize.

What was his problem? Was he worried that the first outing was so successful that he'd never be able to live up to it? Cameron's fear seemed more basic than that—like a swimmer who'd spotted a shark fin. But why? What did he have to be afraid of?

It was frustrating in the extreme. The Positive Action Group was every guidance counselor's dream. I'd been waiting my entire career for something like this. The new members were champing at the bit for the next challenge.

The teachers and administrators wanted more. Audra Klincker had me on speed dial. I was even starting to hear from parents. Everybody wanted to push forward—except for Cameron.

And then, one day, the problem solved itself.

I was unpacking another carton of raffle tickets—sales were still slow, but I was hoping to recruit some of the new P.A.G. members as salespeople. The club's web page was up on my computer, and I noticed something that hadn't been there just a few minutes ago.

> # CALLING ALL PAGGERS
> # NEXT P.A.G. MEETING
> # TUESDAY AFTER SCHOOL
> # IN THE SMALL GYM
> # BE THERE OR BE SQUARE!

My heart soared. Cameron had changed his mind! And, I thought, patting myself on the back just a little, I might have had a little to do with that, with my constant nagging—ahem, counseling.

_____

The next time I saw him, I pumped his arm in congratulation. "You're the best, Cameron! Thanks for doing the right thing!"

"You're welcome, Mr. Fan—uh—sir."

Maybe I'd misjudged the poor kid. He was just shy and superpolite. Nobody called teachers *sir* anymore.

I was up nights brainstorming future projects to suggest. The Sycamore YMCA needed a paint job; the Village Green at the center of town hadn't had a thorough cleanup in years; the local hospital and rehab center were looking for volunteers. There were food drives to be organized, charity fund-raisers to be staffed, fences and signs to be power-washed. Middle schoolers couldn't do it all, of course. But with adult supervision, the Positive Action Group could be a real source of help.

If there was ever a community that needed a boost, it was Sycamore. The word had just come from the Department of Transportation that the rumors were true: Sycamore was losing its freeway exit. It would be a huge blow to the local businesses in town, especially since the nearest ramp drew potential customers right into the big regional mall. I knew that Cameron's family ran a furniture showroom, so for sure the stress of all this had to be affecting the Boxers. It would be practically therapy for him to do something for the town.

I spent all of Tuesday in a state of anticipation. As I approached the small gym, I could hear the buzz of a good crowd inside. Sure enough, a section of bleachers had been set up, and it was almost completely full—seventy or eighty kids at least. That meant we'd attracted even more members than we had since my last count. Very satisfying.

Xavier was there, and to my surprise, he was sitting in the front row, awake and alert. The McBean kid was, too, and this time he'd brought some of his former teammates from the Seahawks. Jordan was also back, with his campaign manager. On the other side of the stands, I spotted Kelly and Jordana, his opponents in the upcoming student council election. Daphne was in the company of several friends as well—hopefully, they weren't all as passionate as she could be.

I saw straight-A students and those who were just squeaking by; drama nerds and cheerleaders and yearbook staffers. What a turnout! Everybody was here—everybody except—

Uh-oh.

I scanned the bleachers again, certain I'd simply missed him. I peered from face to face to face.

There was no Cameron Boxer.

How could he call a meeting, post it on the web page, and then not show up himself?

Heart sinking, I realized I already had the answer: Because he was Cameron Boxer, and with him there didn't have to be a reason.

I ran all through the school, scouring hallways and peering around corners. By the time I pounded up to the second floor, I was bathed in perspiration. I must have looked like a crazy person—hyperventilating, sweat-covered, eyes wild and seeking.

And there he was, standing with Pavel and Chuck, stowing books in a locker that wasn't his.

"Cameron!" I rasped in a voice my own mother wouldn't have recognized. "What are you doing here?"

He slammed the locker door quickly. "Oh, hi, Mr. Fan—uh, sir."

"Don't 'sir' me! Why aren't you at the meeting?"

He seemed completely mystified. "Meeting?"

I lost it. "The Positive Action Group meeting! You can't tell me you don't know about it! It's *your* meeting! You yourself posted it on the web page!"

I went on for a while, venting and raving. I probably would have screamed my head off, except we had a gym full of kids waiting for us. If they gave up on the P.A.G. and walked out, we'd never get them back.

So I dragged the three of them down to the small gym, where all those members—*paggers*, they called themselves now—were sitting expectantly. The instant Cameron walked through the door, they leaped to their feet and cheered.

And how did the P.A.G. president respond to the adoration? He walked a little shorter, his head sunk a little deeper into his shoulders. Almost as if he was hoping that this giant ovation was for somebody else.

I thought back to my college days, when I was training to be a counselor. I'd always envisioned my future students just like this—energized, motivated, united.

Never in a million years could I have imagined anyone like Cameron Boxer.

CHAPTER SEVENTEEN
PAVEL DYSAN

I never thought Cam could get as worked up about anything as he got about video games.

I was technically wrong about that.

"Of course it was you!" he exclaimed right in my face. "You're the one who hacked into the school site in the first place!"

He was talking about the post on the P.A.G. page setting up the second meeting. I was innocent, but I understood why he would suspect me. My web skills were legendary. And besides, who else would it have been?

"I didn't do it, man."

He was red-faced, his eyes practically bulging. This was a guy who got so in the zone that he could ignore a truckload of firemen until they'd axed his door down. "It had to be you! You're the only one with the login information!"

"If I figured it out, other people can, too."

Chuck had a suggestion. "Maybe it was the Friends of Fuzzy. We already know Jennifer Del Rio plays hardball."

Cam shook his head. "It doesn't make sense. Jennifer wants the P.A.G. to stop. Why would she call a meeting so we could plan to do more stuff?"

We had a mystery on our hands. The fact that I hadn't made the post scheduling the new meeting didn't change the fact that *somebody* had. Who? Mr. Fanshaw? Impossible. You couldn't fake the kind of freak-out he'd gone through after Cam didn't show up in the small gym.

But if not him, then who? Jordan, to win votes? String, so he could work his way back onto the football team? Xavier, so he'd have community service to perform? Daphne, because she believed the P.A.G. could help that beaver she was so nuts about?

I was no closer to an answer as Cam's dad drove the three of us and Melody to the P.A.G.'s second project that weekend. Mr. Boxer wasn't in the best mood. The replacement front door had arrived that morning, and it didn't fit.

"It's not advanced science," he seethed. "All you need is a tape measure!"

Technically, measurement was a fairly advanced science, but I didn't get the feeling that Mr. Boxer wanted to hear it.

"At least the P.A.G.'s going great," Melody put in sweetly. "Cam, why don't you tell us about—"

Her brother silenced her with an elbow to the ribs.

We stopped to pick up Katrina. She ignored the open seat with Melody in the middle row and made a point of squeezing in next to Cam in the back. "This is going to be so fun!"

"Picking up garbage," Cam grumbled, leaning into me to get away from her. "Yeah, fun."

As we approached the Village Green, I could see right away that this was very different from our mission at the senior citizens' garden project. A long line of cars stretched ahead of us, dropping off paggers. Daphne greeted the volunteers, checking names against a list on her clipboard. Jordan and Felicia were at her side, handing out trash bags and pointed sticks. When I got mine, I noted that each spike pierced a printed paper that read *VOTE TOLEFFSEN*.

Audra Klincker was there, too, standing with Mr. Fanshaw next to the gazebo. She'd brought a photographer with her this time, so we were definitely going to be in the newspaper again. Cam wasn't going to like that.

Speaking of Cam, everybody wanted a piece of him. They shook his hand, high-fived and fist-bumped him, slapped him on the back, congratulated him.

"Yeah, Cam, this is awesome," Chuck enthused, stabbing wet newspapers and filling his bag. "What a great idea!"

Cam glared at him. "This wasn't my idea. It was

Mr. Fanmail's. I didn't even know about the meeting until we got dragged there."

One voice rose above all others. "Bag's full already! No one picks up garbage like The String!"

His football buddies raced to keep up. The air was a blur of trash and pointed sticks. Coach Branson would faint if he saw it—two-thirds of his precious team poking needle-sharp spikes at each other.

There were a few minor injuries when kids stabbed feet instead of litter. Katrina fell out of a tree she'd climbed to get a plastic bag off a branch. But, luckily, she landed right in Xavier's arms.

A shouting match broke out between some paggers and a group of gardeners with leaf blowers, but they eventually agreed to come back later.

"What a waste," Cam lamented. "A whole day of Rule the World training down the drain. And for what?"

That was when I noticed something I honestly hadn't expected to see. The lawns were lush, green, and well kept. No soda cans or candy wrappers floated in the fountain. The flowerbeds and bushes were litter-free. So were the walkways, the playground, and the band shell.

"Check this place out," I said. "I never realized what a dump it was until I saw it all cleaned up. *We* did that. It wouldn't have happened without us."

"So what?" Cam grunted. "You think all the other

contestants spent the day garbage-picking? They were practicing, like we should have been. Evil McKillPeople is going to merc us."

"Maybe," I acknowledged. "But you can't technically call it a waste. It wasn't what we would have chosen on our own, but it was something good."

He looked at me like I'd just run over his dog.

CHAPTER EIGHTEEN
JENNIFER DEL RIO

The Klincker Kronicle

. . . In the past three weeks, these wonderful, selfless young people have restored our Village Green to its former glory, run a successful toy drive for Sycamore Children's Hospital, and volunteered in the kitchen for Meals on Wheels. If you need proof that there is hope for the next generation, look no further than Cameron Boxer and his Positive Action Group . . .

I heaved the paper across the room so violently that it knocked the Red Bull out of Tony's hands, spraying him.

"Hey, what was that for?"

"The Positive Action Group, the Positive Action Group!" I snarled. "Every toilet in this town is plugged up with the Positive Action Group! If I hear the name Cameron Boxer one more time, I'll scream!"

"You're already screaming," he pointed out.

Poor Tony. He'd been putting up with a lot lately.

I was stressed to the limit. Writing college application

essays did that to a person. Especially when that person's number-one accomplishment—being Grand Pal of the Friends of Fuzzy—was now totally meaningless thanks to a bunch of middle schoolers. They didn't have Harvard to impress. Their lives were all about Girl Scout cookies and Bat Mitzvah lessons and zit cream! Oh, what I wouldn't give to go back to those simpler times—except I was never a Girl Scout, I'm not Jewish, and my skin has always been fine-grained and perfect.

"I explained to Cam Boxer exactly how things work around here. He said he understood me. And what does he up and do? The Positive Action Group is ten times bigger than before! They've got so many kids they have to break them up into separate work crews! How do you compete with people who can paint three different orphanages in the same day?"

Tony had a suggestion. "You know, Jen, why are you getting so bent out of shape about the middle school kids? Wouldn't it be smarter just to come up with some great new stuff for the Friends of Fuzzy?"

I blew my stack. "Name one thing! They've got it all covered! The P.A.G. has cornered the good-deeds market around here! You think I haven't tried? Every time I go to a place to offer our services, it's like, 'No, thanks. The paggers are coming for that.' They're like a disease! I hate them so much!"

"Don't say that," Tony pleaded. "My little brother's in the P.A.G. He doesn't mean any harm. He loves it."

I could not have been more wounded. "And you let this go on? Under your own roof?"

He shrugged. "My folks support it a thousand percent. What am I going to do? Tell them it's keeping my girlfriend out of Harvard?"

Tony was a great guy, tall and easy to look at, with shoulders that seemed to go on forever. But he obviously had a lot to learn about being in a relationship.

Still, this little-brother thing could work to our advantage. It was almost like having an inside man—a spy. We could pick his brains to find out what the P.A.G. was up to next.

That's why, a few days later, Tony was pulling the Charger into a grove of trees at the edge of Ravine Park, a nature preserve that divided the town into East and West Sycamore. We ducked our heads as three large school buses roared past us into the park. The Positive Action Group had gotten so big that it created a traffic jam when parents dropped all the volunteers off. The middle school had to provide buses to get everybody where they needed to be. Didn't that burn your microwave popcorn?

We got out and stole through the underbrush, the whipping branches and jutting twigs scratching at our faces and arms.

"This is crazy, Jen," Tony complained. "Why don't we just walk up to them and ask what they're doing?"

"I refuse to give them the satisfaction. The Friends of Fuzzy were here long before anybody thought of the P.A.G. Farley J. Peachfuzz must be spinning in his grave."

"I don't think Farley J. Peachfuzz was actually real," Tony offered.

"Get down!" I hissed.

We ducked behind a bush overlooking the clearing where the buses were parked. I could see Audra Klincker already waiting there, and—was that the mobile unit of Sycamore Channel Four? Who was next—CNN? Just how famous was the P.A.G. getting? The Friends of Fuzzy practically had to beg for a double-page spread in the high school yearbook.

Then the doors folded open and out poured battalions of middle schoolers, all carrying picks, shovels, sledge-hammers, buckets, and wheelbarrows.

I actually felt my jaw drop. "What are they doing? What did Robbie say?"

Tony shrugged. "I didn't get it. Something about Elvis."

"The *singer*? Is he buried here? Why are they digging him up?"

Eventually, I got so bewildered that I gave up on secrecy and sent Tony down there to ask somebody. He was gone a long time. In the distance, I could hear kids talking excitedly and even laughing. I don't remember myself in middle school but I'm pretty sure I wasn't ever dumb enough or immature enough that slogging through a swamp was my idea of a good time.

I don't know what irritated me more: The fact that the P.A.G. was eating our lunch or the fact that they were having so much fun doing it. Fast-forward to when they were the ones slaving over college applications, and we'd see how much fun they were having.

A giddy voice, louder than the rest, cackled: "You losers might as well go home right now! Nobody digs mud like The String!"

Middle school.

When Tony finally came back, he was splattered with grime. I couldn't read the expression on his face.

"Well?" I prompted.

"They're building a beaver habitat," he told me.

"No, seriously."

"I am serious. That's Elvis—the beaver who's been chewing stuff up around town. He's going to live here."

I started to laugh—not because I thought it was a joke, but because I was really, really happy. Finally the Positive Action Group was making its first mistake. I'd been in the Friends of Fuzzy long enough to recognize a bad good deed, and this was a real stinker. It took a ton of time and man power and resources, and it helped no one except a big rodent with a taste for fence posts. When this got around, Cam Boxer would be ruined, and the P.A.G. with him.

Or so I thought.

When the story came out on TV and in the Klincker Kronicle, it was like a beaver habitat was the greatest thing in the world, and any town that didn't have one might as well set itself on fire.

I DVRed the news and watched it over and over again, each time expecting it to say something different. It never did. The Positive Action Group wasn't dead. It was stronger and more alive than ever!

Tony put a sympathetic arm around my shoulders. "So you were wrong. So what?"

I couldn't tear my eyes from the TV screen. "A beaver lodge! They haven't even got a beaver to live in it. Didn't you hear the announcer? Nobody's seen Elvis for weeks! But, hey, Cam Boxer did it, so it must be perfect."

"When I saw him in Ravine Park, he didn't seem too into it," Tony offered.

"I think," I said through clenched teeth, "that he needs another lesson."

Tony backed away. "I'm not making him walk home from California. He's only a kid. It's not safe."

"We won't touch a hair on his stupid head. I just want to make sure he knows we're watching him."

He knew we were watching him, all right. Every day, when he got out of school, we were parked there. Tony's ride didn't exactly blend into the scenery. It was fire-engine red, with oversize tires and a hole in the muffler, so it sounded like an M1 tank. When Boxer began to walk down the street, we'd parallel him. I'd roll down my window just enough to hang a pom-pom outside—a calling card. If he ran, we'd speed up. I was ready to go even further and park outside his front door. But it turned out he didn't have one—only a sheet of plywood covered in graffiti. Leave it to him.

I wrote *FUZZY IS EVERYWHERE* on it in my favorite lipstick—the one that matches Tony's car.

We were getting to him. There was no question about that. He was starting to go home cutting through people's yards, climbing fences, and skirting pools. But Tony knew the streets pretty well. We always caught up with him.

One time, he stopped dead in his tracks and approached the car. I just glared at him through the glass, so he knocked on the window. When I rolled it down, he said, "I hate the Positive Action Group as much as you do. I only started it to get my parents off my back, and now I can't stop it. Nobody can!"

I honestly could have forgiven him up until that moment. I could even have pictured myself keeping in touch with him from Harvard after he shut down the

P.A.G. to help me get in. But *this*—to look me straight in the eye and lie—was inexcusable. It was the straw that broke the camel's back, the point of no return.

"Drive, Tony."

We peeled away with a screech of tires.

One thing was clear: I could no longer handle this on my own. The P.A.G. had hundreds of volunteers, but they were still just middle schoolers. We were the Friends of Fuzzy, steeped in tradition. It was time to fight for what was ours.

Tony shot me a look. "Why the face? The kid practically apologized. The war's over, right?"

I set my jaw. "The war has just begun."

CHAPTER NINETEEN
CAMERON BOXER

My lifestyle was slipping away, and I didn't know how to get it back.

There were eight hundred fourteen students in our school and six hundred forty-five of them were P.A.G. members. According to Pavel, who did math in his head, that was almost 80 percent. I would have loved to find the other 20 percent and thank them for their nonsupport. But I didn't have time to look for them. I didn't have time for *anything*.

My whole reason for inventing the P.A.G. was so I wouldn't get banned from video games. Now, thanks to the P.A.G., I never got near my console. I was too busy.

Whoever had hacked into the web page was still doing it, posting all this stuff. We had meetings practically every afternoon, and most of them weren't even real meetings. We had Cookie Day and Crazy Hat Day and Pagger Pride Day, where we silk-screened P.A.G. T-shirts. Not showing up wasn't an option. They'd come to get me. It wasn't like before when I only had to worry about Mr. Fanlight and Daphne and a handful of others. Everybody knew me now. I tried to come up with excuses—doctor's appointments, stomachaches, scorpion bites. They thought I was kidding. No one could be as sick as I was pretending to be. No one alive, anyway.

Even Chuck was on my case to attend all these things. Chuck—one of my best friends, who knew better than anybody what an un-thing the P.A.G. was supposed to be. He loved it. Everybody loved it. Everybody except the president.

So I went. But it wasn't just after school. Some mornings, we were called in early. On weekends, we had so many volunteers that we had to break up into separate work crews. There were barely enough projects to go around.

That left just the evenings free. But by the time I was done with homework and could get down to the basement to practice for Rule the World, other things would come up. I got phone calls. Daphne wanted to pick my brains about how we were going to find Elvis to put him into his new home. Like I knew all the beaver hangouts. Katrina texted me from the mall. She needed my opinion on whether or not she should cut her hair. Felicia threw a party so she could hit me up to endorse Jordan in the student council election. The very next night, Kelly held a bash of her own, and tried to strong-arm me into dumping Jordan and backing her. String dragged me to football parties, which offended the soccer players. So I had to go to their parties, too.

Pavel didn't understand why I was so miserable. "What are you complaining about? You're *popular*! All the guys want to hang out with you. All the girls want to date you. You get invited to everything. No one passes gas without asking your permission. What's the downside?"

That bugged me. "What about Rule the World, huh? If I want to get on the console at all, I have to sneak down to the basement at three in the morning! And," I added sarcastically, "I'm sure you and Chuck are getting in tons of practice without me."

"Well," he mumbled, "we're pretty busy with the P.A.G., too."

I was bitter. "The last time I faced Evil McKillPeople, he pinned me in fifteen seconds at extreme wrestling."

"Evil McKillPeople always beats you."

"Yeah, but I usually put up a fight. Don't you get it? I'm *losing* myself. It took thirteen years to build my lifestyle, and the P.A.G. has it leveled to the ground in just a few weeks."

He was sympathetic, but there was nothing he could do to help me. There was nothing I could do to help myself.

When I finally managed to wangle some decent gaming time, my space cruiser had barely entered planetary orbit when the banging began.

"Cam!" came a bellow from outside. *"Are you in there?"*

"Go away," I murmured under my breath. "Please go away."

Even Borje heard it through my microphone, all the way in Sweden. "Your mom isn't baking more ziti today?" he asked nervously.

"Come quick!" shouted the voice. *"It's an emergency!"*

I threw off the headset and sprinted upstairs. At the front door, the plywood vibrated with every pounding blow. *"Cam!"*

"Come to the back!"

I stepped out the kitchen door just in time to see a football player in full equipment wheel around the corner of the house and charge at me at full speed. A split second before he would have flattened me, he stopped short and pulled off his helmet. There, gasping, the black smudges on his cheeks running with sweat, stood String McBean.

"I thought you were off the team," I said lamely.

"The String's been working out with the high school JV squad to get me up to speed. So when I came back to our locker room to get changed, I passed the office, where Mr. Fanshaw was getting bawled out because a bunch of paggers tore up some bushes at the public library."

I had to ask. "Why would they do that?"

"They *didn't*! I was on that library crew. We washed down all the furniture in their outdoor reading garden.

And let me tell you, nobody scrubs pigeon poop like The String—"

"So who ruined the bushes?" I interrupted.

"Nobody!" he insisted. "I mean, *somebody* did it, but it wasn't us paggers. Legit."

I felt the pull of the basement, but something was eating at me. String McBean was only in the Positive Action Group for extra credit so he could return to the football team. What was the skin off his back if we got blamed for a few ripped bushes? Was that really terrible enough to send a guy scrambling all over town in full pads and a helmet?

My thoughts were interrupted by an earsplitting roar.

String jumped. "What the—"

But I'd already recognized the unmuffled engine of a certain Dodge Charger that had been stalking me for more than a week. As we watched, the bright red car came howling down the quiet street doing at least sixty. It slowed in front of the house. The rear window lowered, and something was tossed out onto our lawn. The Charger screeched away, accelerating out of the neighborhood.

We ran over to the mysterious object. It was a clump of bushes, the earth still clinging to torn roots.

At least now I knew who ruined the library's bushes. And why. It was the Friends of Fuzzy, and they'd done it so they could blame it on the P.A.G.

"I've definitely seen that car around," String mused.

Yeah, me too. These days, I saw it in my sleep. "Forget it."

"Forget it?" he exclaimed. "That guy is making everyone think the P.A.G. are the bad guys! Are we going to let him get away with that?"

At that moment, I wanted to scream: *Who cares? Does it kill zombies or help you prestige or level up? Does it earn you a speed boost, or a better weapon, or a magic spell?* Those were supposed to be the things that mattered!

But I couldn't say that to String, so I kept my mouth shut.

He looked angry for a moment, and then his expression slowly turned to understanding. "I get it. We don't sink to that level. The P.A.G.'s too chill for that. We let our reputation speak for itself. Man, respect from The String! No wonder they made you pagger-in-chief."

No wonder.

CHAPTER TWENTY
CHUCK KINSEY

I still liked video games. They just weren't my whole life anymore. Sooner or later, something comes along that shows you what really matters.

That's what being a pagger did for me. Before that, everything was about hanging out with Cam and Pavel, eating gummy worms, and playing video games. Now I had a higher purpose—a calling, almost, although it had nothing to do with church.

I knew it the first minute we were out there at the senior citizens' garden project. This old guy bent over to dig up the last of his potatoes, and his back went out because it had been "wonky," whatever that means, since the Korean War. So I did it for him. It was easy for me. He was smiling. I was smiling. Even one of the potatoes looked like it had kind of a smile on its "face," although that was obviously random. It was a perfect moment, and I did it just by getting down on my hands and knees and pulling a few lumps out of the ground.

It was amazing that I'd lived thirteen years and never really understood about helping before. Yeah, it was good for other people, but it was even better for the guy doing the helping. I should have known that, because my sister, Emma, had been in the Friends of Fuzzy since freshman year of high school. But sometimes you couldn't see the forest for the fire.

I used to get upset when my clan base got sacked, or when Evil McKillPeople crushed me. But now everything was cool, because the P.A.G. had shown me what was important.

Which was why I flipped out when I saw the Klincker Kronicle that morning.

The Positive Action Group has done so much good for this town that it's a shame to hear about the incident at the library last week. We all understand that middle schoolers in their playful high spirits may do some accidental damage. But when sanitation workers found a section of honeysuckle hedge in the garbage outside the home of P.A.G. president Cameron Boxer, it was hard not to conclude that this was an act of deliberate vandalism.

I choked on a bite of toast. "That's not true!"

Emma laughed. "That'll teach your dumb friend to dispose of the evidence in his own trash can. I always knew that kid's head wasn't screwed on right."

"The P.A.G. didn't touch those bushes!" I swore.

"Jennifer Del Rio tore them up and dumped them on Cam's lawn."

My mother frowned. "Jennifer would never do anything like that. She's a lovely girl."

"You're delusional," Emma said to me.

There was something about her face that made me uneasy—an *I-know-something-you-don't* look.

Later, on the way to school, Cam, Pavel, and I passed by the little kids' playground on Fourth Street. A P.A.G. crew had worked there the previous afternoon, power-washing the jungle gym and swing sets.

I stared. The place was a swamp. Mud dripped from the climber and oozed down the twisty slide and the see-saws. There were piles of it on the toddler swings. The sandbox was more like a quicksand box.

We stopped in front of the sign declaring this to be Eagle Park. Right across the face of it, someone had written in magic marker:

MUD IS THICKER THAN WATER
PAGGERS RULE

"Jennifer and Tony did this!" I exclaimed in horror.

"Then it's not our problem," Cam said pointedly.

"It is if Audra Klincker writes in her stupid column that it's our fault," Pavel countered.

"We shouldn't have to think about this," Cam complained. "We're supposed to be in training for Rule the World. We're not going to make it past the first round!"

"Come on, Cam," I pleaded. "You're a pagger, too. I know things didn't turn out the way we planned, but we can't let Jennifer and Tony do this to us!"

He just kept on walking.

At school, everyone was talking about Eagle Park, but also about the flowerbeds in front of the community college. They grew chrysanthemums to spell out *WELCOME ALUMNI* for homecoming weekend. The P.A.G. had weeded the beds just a few days before. Now everything was dead, trampled to pieces, and kicked into the earth.

"Do you think it'll get blamed on us?" I asked.

"Count on it," Jordan predicted grimly. "I saw Audra Klincker over there with a photographer. It's so unfair."

Felicia looked thoughtful. "Unfair or not, I don't think you can risk being a part of this. If it turns into a scandal, Kelly could use it to bury you in the election."

"I'm standing right here," Kelly said in an annoyed tone. "And I'm as P.A.G. as anybody. This is bigger than the election. Somebody's out to get us."

I was dying to tell them what I knew about Jennifer and Tony, but Cam had sworn me to secrecy.

"I'm not going up against Jennifer," Cam insisted. "She's crazy."

"This is too important, man. Hundreds of paggers are depending on you."

He shrugged. "It doesn't matter. I've got no proof."

I pounced on this. "Of course you do! You've got a witness. String was with you when Tony dumped that bush on your lawn."

He laughed without smiling. "I can hear it now— 'Nobody witnesses a bush-dumping like The String!'"

"Cameron!"

Mr. Fanshaw burst out of the stairwell, skidded once on the terrazzo floor, and swooped down on us.

"Hi, Mr. Fan—uh, sir."

"Cameron, what's going on?"

"We can explain about the park!" I burst out. "And the flowerbeds!"

"Never mind that," the guidance counselor exploded. "What about the leaves?"

"Leaves?" Cam echoed.

"The P.A.G. was supposed to rake the leaves around Sycamore House. A crew was put together, and the school provided a bus. What happened?"

I was mystified. "We *did* it. Ask anybody."

"I just drove by there," Mr. Fanshaw snapped. "I saw it with my own eyes."

He was so bewildered that he signed Cam and me out at the office and the three of us drove over to Sycamore House, which was our town's historical society offices and mini-museum. It was the first home ever built around here, back in the early 1800s, and it was surrounded by rolling lawns and ginormous trees. It had taken an entire busload of us nearly four hours to rake and bag all those leaves.

Mr. Fanshaw pulled up to the curb and we stared. The lawn was so deep with leaves that you couldn't even see the grass.

I looked at Cam, and we both understood. Jennifer and Tony could rip up a bush, or stomp on flowers, or maybe even slime a jungle gym. But no two people could do this, not even if they worked all night.

"How do you explain this?" Mr. Fanshaw demanded.

Neither of us answered. What was there to say?

That night, I was taking out the garbage when my dad pulled into the driveway in his pickup. He got out, leaving the motor running. "I'm just going to change," he told me. "I have to go to the car wash. The next time your sister borrows the truck, it would be nice if she didn't trash it." He rushed inside.

Curious, I hopped up on the running board and peered into the payload. Leaves plastered the flatbed and clung to the sides, wet and shredded. There were darker shapes, too—shreds of torn lawn bags.

Suddenly, I knew how Jennifer and Tony had been able to undo all our hard work. They hadn't. Not by themselves, anyway. They'd had help from people like my own sister. High school kids had more freedom than we did. They could stay out later. And they had access to cars and pickup trucks.

Last night they'd driven all the way out to the town dump, loaded up our lawn bags, and brought the leaves back to Sycamore House.

Cam thought he was being picked on by Jennifer and her boyfriend. He didn't know the half of it.

We were under full-on attack from the Friends of Fuzzy.

CHAPTER TWENTY-ONE
DAPHNE LEIBOWITZ

It killed me that Elvis was missing out.

We'd built him a lodge fit for a prince, and now it was standing empty, waiting for him to come and claim it as his own.

Credit to Cam Boxer for the fact that there was any habitat at all. I was positive he'd never let the P.A.G. do anything for Elvis. But I was wrong. He didn't stand in my way at all. His leadership style had a really light touch. I was just starting to appreciate it.

Elvis. That was the tragic part. No one knew where he was. It had been weeks since we'd spotted him at the senior citizens' garden project. And there'd only been one sighting after that—swimming in a storm drain off Main Street after a heavy rain. Since then, nothing.

If it hadn't been for the support of my fellow paggers, I don't know what I would have done. That was another reason I was grateful to Cam: He'd created more than a fantastic club; he'd created a community. By this time, we had over seven hundred members—almost the entire school.

Not everybody was supportive. Xavier said if I wanted to find Elvis, I should "look under the front wheel of the nearest truck." I swatted him with my book bag, which freaked people out, because Xavier had a bad reputation. But he just laughed and told me he was messing with my head.

Well, it was no joke, and Xavier knew it. In her last column, Audra Klincker wrote:

. . . to build a beaver habitat for no beaver would be a hilarious farce if not for the waste of time, man power, and school resources. With our freeway ramp scheduled to be demolished in a matter of weeks, Sycamore could soon be a town with its best days in the rearview mirror. We will be facing tough choices on how we spend our limited resources. And while we can expect no easy answers, it seems clear that unoccupied beaver lodges should be very low on our list of priorities.

What a hypocrite that Audra Klincker was! When we were building the lodge, she was our biggest fan. But that had been back when the P.A.G. was the newest and hottest thing in town. And, even though I hated to admit it, those days were in the rearview mirror, too, just like our freeway exit was going to be.

It was so unfair that the P.A.G. was getting blamed for stuff we didn't even do. We were working harder than ever. With so many members, we practically had to beg people to let us help them, just to keep our paggers involved. But every job we took on, every drive we helped out with, every cleanup we did—something bad always happened, and it wasn't our fault. Either the work went sour, or a shutter or window would get broken, or something rude would get spray-painted on a wall. Sometimes the whole job would be mysteriously undone. Someone was sabotaging us. But who?

We were starting to get bad press, and not just from the Klincker Kronicle. The police chief called us "the middle school wrecking crew." All we'd ever wanted to do was help. That really hurt!

If you thought *we* were upset, you should have seen Mr. Fanshaw. He once told me that he considered the Positive Action Group the greatest achievement in his entire career. He'd backed the P.A.G. from the very beginning when Cam had first proposed it. He was our faculty adviser. A lot of our best projects had been his idea. You couldn't miss the dark circles under his eyes. The poor guy wasn't sleeping, worrying about what was going wrong.

It had to hurt for him to watch our jobs evaporate until almost nobody wanted us anymore. But Mr. Fanshaw never gave up on us. He called in some favors and arranged for the P.A.G. to repaint the pool area at the community Y.

"This is a major opportunity, people," he announced at our next meeting, which had to be held in the double gym with the room divider removed. "It's a big undertaking, and a tough one. But it's also in a high-profile location that half the town goes to. If we can ace it, I know we can turn everything around."

The roar shook the rafters. P.A.G. meetings had become a lot like pep rallies at our school. Bigger, even, now that String was off the Seahawks.

"I'll hand it over to your P.A.G. president, Cameron Boxer!"

This time the cheer was even louder, because everybody stomped on the bleachers at the same time. The whole building seemed to shake.

It took a while to find Cam, so the noise died out a bit. But as soon as he stepped to the microphone, the volume pumped back up.

When it finally got quiet enough for him to speak, he said, "I agree," and the place went nuts again.

It wasn't exactly the Gettysburg Address, but we all understood his message. The P.A.G. was alive and kicking, and the boss was in the driver's seat. He'd never said much about Elvis, either, but when the time had come, Cam had made things happen.

We put thirty-six paggers on the work crew. More than double that showed up at the Y on Saturday morning.

"It's not a bad idea," Mr. Fanshaw decided. "Painting can be messy, so it'll be good to have extra people taping walls and laying drop cloths."

We entered the building, checked in at reception, and made our way to the pool area. That was when the full scope of the mission ahead hit us. The place was massive. There was an Olympic-size pool surrounded by stadium seating; diving boards at low, medium, high, and platform levels; a kiddie pool off to the side with an interactive water park; two hot tubs; and a waterslide. Most of our job was walls and trim, of course, because many of the surfaces were tiled. But it was still an awful lot of work. The paint cans alone, piled four high, covered a giant rolling palette so heavy that Xavier could barely move it.

We got to it. There wasn't much complaining, or even goofing off. We were the Positive Action Group, and this was what we did. We'd tackled tough projects before. This was just another one.

I was proud of us. Tarps were spread; baseboards taped; paints mixed; brushes, rollers, and sandpaper handed out. We were like a well-oiled machine.

I approached Cam. "When you first created the P.A.G., did you ever dream it would be like this?"

His friend Pavel went into such a coughing fit that I had to pound him on the back.

"No," Cam told me honestly. "Never in a million years."

We worked for a couple of hours until Mr. Fanshaw called a break. We all went into the community room and started in on our bag lunches. Mr. Fanshaw ate with us, but left halfway through to pick up a huge order of Munchkins for dessert. We sent him on his way with a big cheer. We were tired, but happy. The work was going well. There was no feeling quite as satisfying as seeing that your efforts were paying off.

As usual, String was bragging that he'd painted faster, better, and more than anybody else. Several of the guys decided to challenge this, so they trooped back into the pool area. A handful of us followed to serve as judges.

We hadn't even crossed the hall yet and we could already hear that something was different. There was a churning-water sound, a kind of bubbling roar. Xavier threw open the double doors.

We saw the hot tubs first. The whirlpools were on full tilt, and out of the baths rose two pillars of soapsuds, ten feet high and growing. Beyond that, in the interactive water park, a broad-shouldered high school boy in a black leather jacket was emptying a bottle of dishwashing liquid into the kiddie pool.

"Tony?" Cam blurted.

Startled, Tony dropped the bottle, turned tail, and ran.

"Stop him!" shouted half a dozen voices.

String ran him down from behind and tackled him. The two hit the tile floor and slid in a shower of yellow, pale blue, and purple—I blinked—just the same colors as—

That was when I pushed my way forward through the crowd, and saw them. There were at least twenty high school kids, and they were wrecking our work—spilling our paint cans, dumping detergent into all the pools, and writing on the freshly painted walls.

"Stop it!" shouted Chuck.

"Who's going to make us?" jeered an older girl.

I didn't know a lot of high schoolers, but I recognized her immediately. It was Jennifer Del Rio. And as soon as I saw her there, it all came together for me like puzzle pieces locking into place. The Friends of Fuzzy! They'd been the ones dogging us all along, because they couldn't stand to share the spotlight. And now they were here to ruin our biggest project of all.

The other teenagers joined Jennifer, advancing on us menacingly.

"Where's Boxer?" Jennifer's laser-guided eyes locked on Cam in the middle of our group. Tony and two other big guys started toward the P.A.G. president.

"Somebody *do* something!" pleaded Katrina.

There was a loud crunching sound as Xavier pulled the long slide free of its frame and swung it around, sweeping the high schoolers into the big pool. There they flailed in the sudsy, paint-stained water, howling in outrage, windmilling their arms, and kicking up even more foam.

It was so chaotic, so crazy, that I almost missed it. Right in the middle of the struggling teenagers, another head broke the surface of the water—a smaller one, brown and furry, with two large buckteeth.

I heard my own scream as if it were coming from someone else. No wonder nobody had seen Elvis for all these weeks! Somehow, the poor little guy had broken into the Y and was holed up here, living in and out of the pools and hot tubs!

As I watched, one of the boys grabbed Elvis around the midsection, holding him up in triumph. "Hey, it's the missing rat!"

Elvis struggled, his broad flat tail beating at the surface of the water, a beaver's distress signal. At the sight of him looking so frightened, the Y winked out for an instant to be replaced by a furious red haze. The next thing I knew, I was flying through the air. I hit the pool with a mighty splash and began freestyling to the rescue. I heard more splashes all around me, and suddenly there were paggers in the water, swimming into battle—Xavier, String, Chuck, Jordan, donuts—

Donuts?

"Get out of the water!" bellowed Mr. Fanshaw, arms

thrashing. "Get out of the—" And then he sank like a brick.

The dilemma almost tore me in two—should I save Elvis or Mr. Fanshaw? In the end, I had to go with our faculty adviser. I knew Elvis could swim. I wasn't so sure about Mr. Fanshaw.

I dove down, grabbed the guidance counselor's arm, and brought him to the surface. He tried to thank me, but he was spitting up too much water. By now, everybody was in the pool, even Cam, although I think he might have been pushed in. Soggy Munchkins bobbed all around us.

"Where's the beaver?" I shrieked at the high school boy.

He could only shrug.

I did a desperate three-sixty, and nearly let go of Mr. Fanshaw. My eyes fell on a half-open door to the outside.

Elvis had left the building.

CHAPTER TWENTY-TWO
MR. FANSHAW

When I was nine, my mother wanted to put me in swimming lessons. I refused. It was a skill I would never need. I was going to be a teacher, and stay forever on dry land, I argued. If I had known then that I would one day owe my life to Daphne Leibowitz, that would have been a very different conversation.

I still had no idea what made me jump in the water, taking three hundred Munchkins with me. On what level did I not know I was going straight to the bottom? But I'd just left a beautiful example of young people involved in public service work, and returned to the spectacle of an aquatic brawl being fought in mountains of multicolored bubbles. Or maybe it was this: My students were younger and smaller—except maybe Xavier—and they were being threatened. Was I proud of them for finding the courage to stand up for themselves and the good work they were trying to accomplish? You bet! Was I sorry that the Y got trashed and was going to be unusable for at least six months? Well, okay, that too.

The worst part of all was that the Positive Action Group was getting blamed for everything while those bullies and jerks from the high school were being let off scot-free. Audra Klincker wrote in her column that the whole incident had been the high schoolers trying to prevent the P.A.G. from vandalizing the Y. Now the Friends of Fuzzy were earning the gratitude of the community by volunteering to clean up the mess in the pool area that *they'd* made.

My colleague Barbara Lederer wasn't as sympathetic as I'd expected. "It's your own fault," she told me. "You were the one who called Audra Klincker in the first place. You were more than happy with all the publicity you got when she was writing good things about the P.A.G."

"But the good things were all true!" I reasoned. "This is wrong! Those Fuzzies aren't heroes! They came to spoil our job. They've been doing it for weeks!"

"Audra Klincker is a reporter," she explained patiently. "She follows the story. The story used to be how great you are. But nobody wants to read the same thing over and over again. So the story had to change."

I was speechless.

"Plus," she added, "Audra Klincker is an idiot. You're not from around here, but the locals all know that."

Dr. LaPierre was beyond furious. "Do you have any idea how this reflects on the school?"

"Of course I do. But our kids are innocent."

"Well, the high school says *their* kids are innocent."

I was resentful. "The high school is lying. Ask yourself what those teenagers were doing at a closed pool, knowing full well that someone else would be working there. They've been stalking us for a while now. If you'd just take the time to investigate—"

"I don't want it investigated," he interrupted. "I want it over. Shut it down."

I stared at him.

"The Positive Action Group. It's gone."

I was horrified. "Don't they deserve a chance to clear their name?"

"I just came from a demonstration of what waterlogged donuts can do to a seventy-thousand-dollar pool-filtration system. Shut it down."

I begged for mercy. "But it's been so good for our kids! The shy ones have made friends. The young ones aren't intimidated by the upperclassmen anymore. Working side by side has done that for them. Take a boy like Xavier. He hasn't been in trouble once since joining the P.A.G."

The principal's lip curled. "Not unless you consider ripping apart a giant water slide and using it to assault twenty people 'trouble.'"

"Or Freeland," I continued gamely. "He never had a thought beyond the football field. Now he has a real life, and his grades are improving. And what about Cameron Boxer himself? He barely left a footprint in this school. Did you ever think we'd see such leadership from him?"

He held up a hand, policeman-style. "Save your breath. I'm not saying it wasn't good for a while. But it isn't good anymore. End it."

And that was it. I had a lot of good arguments left, but he didn't want to hear them. Dr. LaPierre was my boss. He'd given me a direct order. All that remained was for me to tell seven hundred twenty-nine paggers that they couldn't be paggers anymore.

Well, obviously I couldn't personally break the news to seven hundred twenty-nine people. And I certainly didn't want to deliver a shock like that over the PA. So I paged Cameron.

It was a testament to how much the P.A.G. had become a part of my life that I wasn't even surprised when he didn't show up. A check of my watch gave me a pretty good idea of where he had to be. I left my office, stepping over the boxes of unsold raffle tickets, and made my way to the second-floor boys' room. Sure enough, there was the P.A.G. president, slouched against the sink, phone in hand, playing that game he loved so much—something about clans.

"Cameron?" I said gently. I startled him, and he nearly dropped his phone in the process of fumbling it out of sight.

"Oh, hi, Mr. Fan—uh—sir. I was just—"

"It's all right. I'm not going to report you." It might have been his legendary politeness that made me overlook his cell phone violation. Or maybe it was my heavy heart at what I had to tell him. "I've got bad news, Cameron, and I wanted you to be the first to know so you can pass it on to all the other members. The Positive Action Group is canceled. It's not going to be allowed to operate anymore."

I watched his face as he digested my words. A grimace appeared that sent the corners of his mouth shooting up toward his ears. If I didn't know better, I'd have sworn it was a huge, Grinch-like grin. He was working very hard to keep his emotions in check.

"It was wonderful while it lasted," I went on. "I can't tell you how much I admire what you did for this school. But it's over. I'm sorry."

His tight control never wavered. "Okay."

"Okay," I echoed. It seemed like more should be said, but Cameron had always been a man of few words. Fine, we'd do it his way. We shook hands, and I left him there without ordering him back to class. The kid deserved a little time and space to collect his thoughts.

The last thing I heard as the bathroom door closed behind me was the flourish of trumpets from his video game.

CHAPTER TWENTY-THREE
CAMERON BOXER

When was it ever better than this?

The Positive Action Group was history, so I had my life back. Mom and Dad still gave me credit for creating it, though. And sympathy, too, because I'd been wronged, and my greatest achievement had been taken away from me. Even Melody was cutting me some slack. It was pretty ill.

Better still, I didn't have to worry about Jennifer and Tony anymore. The Friends of Fuzzy were back in business, and they were getting things all their own way. But since I was, too, it didn't bother me that they didn't really deserve it. I'd seen the Dodge Charger a couple of times, but now it just drove right by me. One time I could have sworn I got a friendly wave from Tony behind the tinted window. I'd never realized just how nervous that car had made me. Now it was like when I was five and the family with the big mean dog moved away.

Illest of all, though—I was back on the couch, in the spot perfectly formed for my butt, practicing for Rule the World. Gone were the days of stealing ten minutes here, fifteen minutes there because the P.A.G. was taking up all my time.

I was in the lead chariot, racing around the Circus Maximus, well ahead of the pack, when my wingman, Gaius Magnus, let go of the reins and coasted to a stop.

"Chuck, what are you doing?" I howled, watching his avatar being trampled into the dirt by every other team in the race.

"This is boring," he told me over the headset. "I don't want to play anymore."

"What do you mean 'boring'?" I demanded. "We love this game."

A tone indicated that Chuck had logged out.

"What's with him?" I complained to Pavel after the race was over.

Pavel sounded exasperated over the network. "You've got tunnel vision about your so-called lifestyle," he accused. "You never think about other people and what makes them tick."

"That's kind of harsh," I complained.

"Chuck loved the P.A.G., and he's really bummed about it."

"The P.A.G.?" I echoed. "What does the P.A.G. have to do with video games?"

"Nothing," he replied readily. "There were no chariots, or space aliens, or titans. But when we helped somebody, that person's life was better, even if it was only in a tiny way. And it was in reality, not on any screen. So when

159

Chuck said the game was boring, he technically didn't mean it was a bad game. He just meant it didn't measure up to the stuff we did with the P.A.G. And you know what? I think I agree with him."

I couldn't have been more shocked if he'd told me that *he* was a space alien about to blast me into Dimension X. It had always been Pavel, Chuck, and me, as long as I could remember. The Awesome Threesome! All at once, I felt like I didn't know those guys anymore.

"What about Rule the World?" I asked.

"It'll be fun. I hope you pick me to be your partner. But to be honest, it doesn't seem that important anymore." Well, I must have gasped, because he added, "It's not like we're going to win or anything. If Evil McKillPeople can beat us so easily, there must be plenty of others who can, too. I'll bet there are gamers who are better than *him*."

So I wasn't free of the P.A.G. after all. It was haunting me from beyond the grave.

I abandoned the Circus Maximus early, even offering it to Melody.

She peered at the screen. "Have you figured out the hack where you have a centurion ride beside you? It helps fight off the barbarians in the home stretch."

"What do you know about it?" I said sulkily.

"Katrina and I have been playing a lot lately, now that the P.A.G.'s gone. We kind of miss it, you know."

I ran upstairs.

The P.A.G. haunted me at school, too. String stopped me in the hall to tell me his academic probation was over and he was back on the Seahawks. He reached out his long arms and enfolded me in a bear hug.

"The String owes you, Cam! No P.A.G., no extra credit, no football. Paggers forever!"

He wasn't the only one. All day long, people kept coming up to me with emotional stories about what the Positive Action Group meant to them.

"I never had any friends until the P.A.G."

"We saved that old lady's life."

"Helping people made me feel so good!"

"I met my girlfriend on the day we built the beaver lodge."

"The only time I didn't fight with my brother was when we were on a crew together."

"The Friends of Fuzzy are the bad guys, not us!"

"It's no fair that they broke us up!"

Daphne was especially bitter because Elvis had not been seen since the incident at the Y. "Those high school criminals did this! Elvis would be in his habitat if it weren't for them!"

"Or maybe he'd still be at the Y," I suggested. "It could have been the fight that scared him out."

"What difference does that make?" she lamented. "He's gone now. And we don't even have the P.A.G. to help find him and get him back!"

Beaver-finding had never been the P.A.G.'s job, as I remembered it. But that was happening with everybody. Now that the club was gone, they were remembering it wrong, like we'd done everything short of curing the common cold.

In the cafeteria, I found Jordan and his election opponent Kelly having lunch together.

"The vote's off," Jordan told me cheerfully. "Kelly and I have decided to share the top job and be co-presidents, with Jordana serving as treasurer."

"And we owe it all to you, Cam," Kelly added.

"To *me*?"

"We were wasting so much energy tearing each other down," Jordan confessed. "But in the P.A.G., you showed us the power of cooperation."

Kelly looked anxious. "Do you think they'll let us restart the club once we're in office?"

"I don't know," I told them. "Mr. Fanfare seemed pretty

definite that we were shut down. I think it came straight from the principal."

It was like that nonstop. Ex-paggers pulling me aside to reminisce about "the good old days," and to complain that we got busted up when the Friends of Fuzzy were still going strong. Some even wanted to know what kind of revenge I was plotting.

One thing that was common to everyone—they wanted to know how *I* was handling this terrible disaster. After all, the Positive Action Group was *my* baby.

What could I tell them? That I felt great, like someone had lifted a thousand-pound weight off my back? That for the first time since this P.A.G. stuff started, I was free? That it was all I could do to stop myself from dropping to my knees and thanking the heavens above for releasing me from this monster I'd created?

So I said, "I'm hanging in there." Everyone accepted that.

I was on my way to last period when the door of the supply closet next to my health class opened. An arm reached out, clamped around my neck in a semi–choke hold, and hauled me inside. The door slammed behind me.

I struggled to get away, and when the hold finally relaxed, I wheeled. I was expecting to see Tony and Jennifer there to tie me up and leave me in here, or stuff me in a locker, or chop me into fish bait and dump me in the ocean. You never knew with those two.

Instead, I found myself looking up into the huge features of Xavier Meggett. An icy chill ran up and down my spine, radiating outward to frost my entire body. We were used to Xavier now, but he was still the scariest kid in the school. The P.A.G. was his court-ordered community service. What if, now that we were shut down, he had to go back to juvie? And what if he was blaming me for that?

"Been looking for you all day," he rumbled, glaring down at me with burning eyes.

"Oh, yeah?" My voice sounded squeaky, an octave higher than normal.

"I've got something for you."

Here it comes, I thought in agony. *A punch in the face, a broken arm, a ruptured spleen—*

He pressed something into my hands. When I dared to look down, I found myself holding a roundish, toilet-paper-wrapped object a little bigger than a softball. There was something solid and heavy inside.

"Open it up," he urged.

I don't know what I expected to find in there—a bomb? A shrunken head? My hands were shaking as I tore through the wrapping.

It was a ceramic dish decorated with a pattern of cactus plants. "A bowl?" I croaked.

"Not *any* bowl," he corrected me. "A salsa bowl. But you can also use it for guacamole or con queso dip." I guess I seemed totally clueless, so he added, "I made it in art class."

"Really?" I was impressed. The shape was even, and the cacti were really well painted. It looked like something professional, from a store. I glanced at his hands. They were the size of, like, hams. I couldn't imagine his sausage fingers creating something as nice as this.

"It's really good, but—why are you giving it to me?"

His eyes blazed into mine. "I never finished anything before. Not until the P.A.G. In the P.A.G., we finished *everything* we started. And when we were done, stuff was different. Not just different. Better. If it worked with the P.A.G., it could work other places, too. So this is yours."

"I really like it," I said, and meant it. A salsa bowl was a useful accessory for a gamer. I could already picture it on the table next to my couch in the basement. What were the odds that the least likely person in Sycamore would give me the perfect gift for my lifestyle? "Hey, Xavier, you're not in trouble, are you? You know, because the P.A.G. was your community service, and now . . ." My voice trailed off.

To my amazement, a gigantic tear bubbled out of his left eye and trailed down his massive cheek. I could barely manage the words. "They're not making you go back to—you know, back *there*?"

He wiped his face. "Nah, they cleaned my slate."

"So why . . . ?"

He shook his big head. "I can't explain it. When we had the P.A.G., I woke up in the morning and the day was *about* something! I had something to do, and it was important. Now—it's like I'm just killing time."

"Do you play video games?" I suggested timidly.

He looked at me like I was from another planet. "Not the same," he said sadly. "I don't know if anything can ever be the same again."

CHAPTER TWENTY-FOUR
DR. LAPIERRE

It was my secretary who first called my attention to it.

"Dr. LaPierre, I thought the Positive Action group was disbanded."

"It is," I confirmed. "All their activities have been canceled, and their web page has been taken down. It's as if the club never existed, which is fine with me."

"I see," she said in a confused tone that communicated the exact opposite. She didn't see at all.

"Is there a problem, Carol?" I asked.

In reply, she slid her laptop in front of me on my desk. I immediately recognized the design of the school website. And the page itself?

ARE WE GOING TO TAKE THIS LYING DOWN?

Dr. LaPierre had no right to close us up for what the Friends of Fuzzy did.

Paggers unite!

We need to fight for our rights!

I remained calm. Principals did not panic.

"Carol," I said, "page Cameron Boxer."

The announcement went out over the PA. I waited five minutes, then ten. No sign of the Boxer kid.

"Carol, get Peter Fanshaw in here."

He was already spouting excuses when he entered my office. "I know we haven't sold even a fraction of the tickets, but if we—"

"Never mind the raffle." I swiveled the laptop so that he could see the screen. "What's the deal with this?"

Principals didn't panic; guidance counselors did. "But that's impossible! The P.A.G. is disbanded!"

"Apparently," I told him, "not everybody thinks so. And your Cameron Boxer didn't respond to my page."

He shrugged. "Well, yeah—wait a minute! You think Cameron posted that?"

"I'm all ears if you have another suspect. Go find Boxer and bring him here."

I cooled my heels while Peter tracked the boy down. I had paperwork to do, but I just couldn't concentrate until this issue was settled once and for all. When a principal makes a decision to close a school club, it shouldn't take two tries to have it happen. That web page was a direct challenge to my authority.

When Cameron was right there in front of me, I didn't pull any punches. "Exactly what do you think you're doing?"

I had to give him credit. He was a good actor. He honestly looked like he had no idea what I was talking about. And when I showed him the web page, the shock on his face seemed completely real. There was an Oscar in that kid's future.

"Well?" I prodded.

"I didn't do it," he swore.

I wasn't buying that. "Maybe you didn't do the actual web design, but *you're* the P.A.G."

He shook his head. "There *is* no P.A.G. I shut it down, like Mr. Fan—like *he* said."

Peter spoke up. "Cameron, this is no joke. We need the truth. If you didn't do this, you have to tell us who did."

"I don't know who did it," he said.

I had no patience for that. "You don't seem to realize the amount of trouble you're in right now, Cameron. Take a moment to think about how it will feel to be suspended from school. Think about the conversation I'll be having with your parents. Think about the black mark this will leave on your permanent record."

He regarded me in abject misery. "I'm telling the truth. I don't know who put that on the website, and I don't know how to find out. It was happening before, too—these extra events and meetings would get called, and I wasn't calling them. I know it seems like I was a big shot in the group, but I really didn't do anything. I just started it, and other people took over. They loved it more than me then, and they miss it more than me now. It must be one of them who's doing this. But how will I ever know which one?"

I'd always thought Cameron Boxer was an unimpressive, unmotivated, lazy student. Now I knew better. He was a brilliant schemer and tactician. Not only had he avoided the blame, but he'd found a way to push it off on more than seven hundred former club members. He'd given me so many suspects that he'd effectively given me none at all. How could I ever interrogate 90 percent of my school to get to the bottom of this?

Well, he wasn't going to get away with it. If he thought he could bamboozle John LaPierre the way he'd bamboozled his hordes of followers, Cameron Boxer had picked the wrong principal.

CHAPTER TWENTY-FIVE
PAVEL DYSAN

Cam was pretty ticked off at us. Technically, I understood. He thought when the P.A.G. went away, everything would go back to normal, that our lives would be the way they were before, where everything orbited video games and Rule the World and fun. He didn't see that the P.A.G. had changed Chuck and me. The P.A.G. had changed everybody—everybody except Cam himself. How weird was it that the one guy who was immune was the guy who'd started the whole thing?

Collecting coins, or health points, or trophies on a screen just didn't measure up to the feeling of accomplishment the P.A.G. gave us. And anyway, thanks to Rule the World, Cam had turned into such a tyrant that video games were no fun at all. How could you play at a life-and-death struggle with someone who was treating it like a *real* life-and-death struggle? Whenever one of us got tired, or made a mistake, or if Evil McKillPeople wrecked us, he'd go ape. Even when we were eating gummy worms at Sweetness and Light, he was always lecturing us on some new strategy he wanted us to try. He was working so obsessively at his lifestyle that he wasn't living it.

I felt bad for him—until about four days after the end of the P.A.G., when he came roaring down on me in the stairwell at school.

"It was you!" he raged. "From the very beginning! I should have known!"

I was mystified. "What are you talking about?"

"I just came from LaPierre's office, where I got chewed out for posting things on the P.A.G. web page!"

"There *is* no P.A.G. web page. They took it down."

"Like you don't know!" he accused. "You're the one who put it back up again, just like you're the one who called all that extra stuff! I'll bet you invented Pagger Pride Day, didn't you?"

"No!" I was so shocked I could hardly defend myself. "We talked about this! We settled it!"

"Because you *lied*!" he sputtered. "It's been you the whole time! And now you're posting stupid things like *Are we going to take this lying down?* You're starting a revolution, and it's getting blamed on me! I could get suspended! My parents are being called right now!"

"How can you think I would do something like that?"

"Who created that stupid web page in the first place?" he shot back.

"I did," I replied, "because my *best friend* asked me to."

"But you didn't stop there, did you? You couldn't let the P.A.G. die a natural death. You had all the codes and

172

passwords. You set up meetings every time the wind blew so we always had a bunch of projects going. But even that wasn't enough for you. You had to get cute! Pagger Pajama Day! The Hula-Hoop Marathon for Charity! Win a Dream Date with String McBean!"

"I didn't—"

He cut me off. "And now you're going to get me kicked out of school!"

I pleaded with him. "How long have we been friends? How long have we been the Awesome Threesome? Why would you think I'd do something like that to you?"

"I didn't think you'd bail on Rule the World, either," he seethed. "I didn't think you'd take a fake club and turn it into the meaning of life!"

"It wasn't me," I said earnestly. "I'm not the only person who's ever hacked into a website, you know. All it takes is a password. Maybe you wrote it on something and left it lying around school."

"I never brought it to school."

"Or Dr. LaPierre exposed it. Or somebody else working on the school site."

"Or maybe it was you," he retorted angrily. "Because video games weren't enough for your superbrain. We started the P.A.G. to save Rule the World, but the wheels were turning in your head even then. If Daphne could use it to help a beaver, what could the great Pavel Dysan do?

And if you had to hang me out to dry, well, that's just—that's just—"

"Collateral damage?" I spat.

He took a step toward me, and I took a step toward him. For a minute there, we were right in each other's grills, and it seemed like we were going to settle this the primitive way. That was about as un-Cam as you could get, and definitely un-me. For guys like us, no disagreement was ever so big that it couldn't be resolved with alien warriors at high noon (which technically happened twice a day, since their home planet had a binary sun).

I spun on my heel and walked away, knowing in my heart that we'd lost a lot more than just the Positive Action Group.

CHAPTER TWENTY-SIX
FREELAND MCBEAN

The scoreboard painted the whole picture, and it wasn't pretty. We were down 31–26 to New Albany, with only twelve seconds still on the clock. Coach and Mr. Fanshaw had been as good as their word, getting me reinstated to the Seahawks in time for the postseason. But that would all be for nothing if we lost today. If we couldn't beat New Albany, we'd drop out of the last playoff spot. What was the point of having The String back if there were no games left for me to star in?

On the sidelines, the guys looked terrified. I was the most terrified. One play left, forty-six yards between us and the end zone. Even the cheerleaders knew that the ball would be going to The String. The other team knew it, too, so I was going to be quadruple-covered, mugged, and run over by the New Albany bus. Believe it or not, there were some miracles even I wasn't capable of.

During our last time-out, Coach's pep talk sounded more like the speech you make right before you clean out your locker because the season just ended. He didn't think we could do this any more than we did.

But then he said something none of us expected.

"I see you guys rolling your eyes when I talk about Sycamore pride, but I've got some news maybe you haven't heard yet: The Department of Transportation has set the date for the demolition of our exit ramp—this Saturday, eight a.m. A lot of people think it's going to be the beginning of the end of our way of life here in town. Well, we might not be able to stop the Division of Highways, but we can make a statement on this field, today, right now. And that statement is that Sycamore is *never* out of it so long as we believe in ourselves!"

I wasn't usually big on motivational speeches. You didn't win football games with rah-rah; you won by having somebody awesome like The String on your team and maybe a halfway decent quarterback who could throw the ball in my general direction. But in this case, it really worked wonders for our players. The lights were coming on behind all those desperate eyes. Face guards turned up from the turf. There were twelve seconds left, not zero.

And one of us was The String. Remember that part.

As I lined up wide left, New Albany had a corner and a safety on me, but all the d-backs were looking my way. Whatever happened on this final play, I wouldn't be lonely. I was going to draw a crowd.

"Hike!" barked Ziggy, our quarterback.

I took off down the sideline, and the crowd came with me—corners, safeties, even a linebacker. I peeked over my shoulder and caught sight of the ball coming my way. Coach's freeway ramp speech must have really gotten to Ziggy, whose family ran the local Sunoco station. The pass was about as good as you were going to get from his arm.

The New Albany guys matched me stride for stride, bumping me, grabbing at my jersey, trying to knock me out of bounds. They were bigger, stronger, taller, and had longer arms.

Those poor guys, I thought to myself. *They don't know they're outnumbered.*

There were five of them and only one of me.

But I'm The String and they're not.

My cleats left the field, and I soared higher than I've ever soared before—and that was really saying something. The instant the ball touched my fingertips I knew I had it. But the goal line was still ten yards away, and we had no time-outs left. If I allowed myself to be tackled, the clock would run out.

I schooled them all—stiff-armed one, hurdled another, and beat the rest with sheer blazing speed. When I entered the end zone, I spiked the ball so hard that it left a crater in the ground. Nobody spiked harder than The String.

The entire stadium bugged. Our fans stormed the field to celebrate the last-second, come-from-behind victory. This may have been a crummy, disappointing, mediocre season with The String on academic probation, but now we were back, and play-off bound.

The guys lifted me up on their shoulders. Coach was right there with them, tears streaming down his cheeks, which were bright pink. The chant rang out, not just from our cheerleaders, but from hundreds of throats:

"*String!* . . . *String!* . . . *String!* . . . *String!* . . ."

I drank it in. It was the greatest triumph of my life. At least—it *should* have been.

And it was good. Don't get me wrong. The String was born for moments like this. It just wasn't—*that* good. Something was missing. But what?

What could be better than this—an amazing play only you could make, to score a winning touchdown, with no time remaining, and all the odds against you?

And then it came to me. When the P.A.G. was power-washing the aluminum siding on the outside of the Early Childhood Center two weeks ago, I noticed that the front gutters were clogged with leaves. So Xavier boosted me up and I cleared them out. Nobody cleaned gutters like The String.

Anyway, the very next night, we had this humongous rainstorm. The principal of the center said that if those gutters had backed up, it would have flooded out their front playroom, where they kept all the toys and the pillows and blankets for naptime. From then on, every time I passed that place and saw kids playing in the front room, I'd smile to myself and think: *That was us. This game of Candy Land is courtesy of the P.A.G. This nap brought to you by The String and his fellow paggers.* We didn't save them from a burning building, or protect them from a pack of attacking yetis. But those kids' lives were a little better because of *us*.

The chants of *"String! . . . String! . . . String! . . ."* went in one ear and out the other. I'd won the game, and that was great. We were in the play-offs. We might even win it all.

But so what?

The String used to be part of something *off the chain*— something that wasn't just numbers on a scoreboard. The P.A.G. made a *difference*.

And we just let it go like it was nothing.

"Guys!" I shouted. "Put me down!" The celebration was so loud and crazy that they couldn't even hear me. I had to wriggle myself back to the field as if I was breaking tackles again.

"You're the man, String!" cried Ziggy, hugging me.

"Of course I'm the man!" I howled back. "Now get out of my way! I've got someplace I need to be!"

I charged around the stadium, staring into faces, desperate to find Cam Boxer. I accepted a lot of high fives, and everybody slapped at my helmet and shoulder pads.

"Cam!" I bellowed. "Has anybody seen Cam?"

"He's not here," came a voice behind me.

I wheeled to face Chuck. His friend Pavel was with him.

"Great catch, String," Pavel told me.

"Never mind that! Where's Cam?"

They both looked completely blank.

"Where is he?" I pressed. "You guys are always together!"

Pavel shuffled uncomfortably. "We had a fight. He's kind of mad at us. Especially me."

"We need him!" I snapped. "We've got to get the P.A.G. back together."

"We can't," Chuck said sadly. "Dr. LaPierre killed the P.A.G. It came straight from the top."

"You're right," I agreed. "*We* can't. We're not the ones who created the P.A.G. out of nothing and turned it into the best thing this school ever had! We need Cam! If anyone can figure out a way to save the P.A.G., it's him!"

They looked at each other. Pavel heaved a sigh. "String, what would you say if I told you that Cam doesn't even care about the P.A.G.? That he's happy it's over?"

"I'd say you're nuts."

"It's true," Chuck confirmed. "It was never supposed to be anything. He only invented it to make his parents think he was getting involved."

"It was just a hoax that got out of control," Pavel added.

The story those guys told me was beyond unbeliev-able, even if I'd paid attention through the whole thing. Sometimes a little A.D.D. could be good for you—like when you played a sport where a split second was the dif-ference between winning and losing. Or when you were being fed a load of garbage about burnt noodles and how the one guy you looked up to was a slacker who only wanted to dweeb out in front of video games.

Or when you were told that the greatest thing you'd ever been part of was a scam.

I felt like they'd punched me. Nobody punched The String.

I scowled at them. "Maybe I'm just some dumb jock. But I know this: The P.A.G. was epic, and it only happened because of Cam. Some friends you turned out to be!"

"We're not lying," Pavel pleaded.

"Get out of my stadium."

Anybody who could stab Cam Boxer in the back didn't deserve to be on the same field as The String.

CHAPTER TWENTY-SEVEN
CAMERON BOXER

It was ill—even knowing that Evil McKillPeople was out there somewhere, waiting to pounce.

The planet was in ruins, its capital city ablaze, which burned magenta because of the chemical content of the atmosphere. Our fleet had ringed the alien world with orbiting lasers, careful to avoid the clouds, which were made of pure nitroglycerine vapor and would explode on contact. It was total victory. All that remained was to capture the insectoid president and remove his scepter of office, which was surgically implanted in his thorax.

I leaned forward on the basement couch, my thumb quivering over the button that would launch the final assault.

"Waiting for your command," said Borje in my ear.

Would you believe it? I shut the game off. It was nothing against Borje. I thought about the voices that were missing—Pavel's, Chuck's—and it just wasn't good anymore.

Are you crazy? I wanted to scream at myself. *You're on the verge of beating the entire game! With Evil McKillPeople on the other side! His gamer tag is right up there on the list of opponents! Take him out! Next stop, Rule the World . . .*

It was no use. The lifestyle I'd worked thirteen years to perfect was in worse shape than the alien surface on the screen—trashed and smoldering, about to be blasted into vapor and sucked down the nearest black hole.

It was all because of that stupid ziti. If only I'd heard Mom and taken it out of the oven, I never would have had to invent the Positive Action Group in the first place. The P.A.G.—that was why Chuck wasn't talking to me and why I wasn't talking to Pavel. And it was why Dr. LaPierre was calling my parents. It hadn't happened yet, but every time the phone rang my head practically exploded.

I could tell Mom and Dad that I wasn't the person riling everybody up on the illegal P.A.G. web page. But they were sure to ask questions, and eventually I would have to lie to cover up the fact that I didn't care about the P.A.G. and never had.

Or I could protect my other lies by lying again and confessing to the web page. But then I'd be copping to something I didn't even do.

No. There was only one way out of this mess: I was going to have to abandon my principles and resort to honesty. It wasn't me, but desperate times called for desperate measures.

A lump formed in my throat, something roughly the size of a bowling ball. I hadn't created the P.A.G. just for giggles, you know. I'd been defending my gaming system and my lifestyle. When I came clean to Mom and Dad, I had to figure they'd nix my sweet setup in the basement, and that might be just for starters.

My eyes traveled from the controller in my hand to the darkened screen to the console itself. They were all turned off. That had been my choice—in the middle of the best part of my favorite game, minutes from the ultimate victory. I'd never done that, not ever. Not even while fire axes were breaking down our front door. That had to mean something.

I dropped the controller like it was white-hot and went upstairs in search of my parents. They were in the front hall admiring the new door and complaining that Sycamore Sanitation hadn't taken away the old plywood, which was still leaning up against our empty trash cans at the curb. Oh, how I wished it was gone. The surface was covered in graffiti, most of it about how awesome the P.A.G. was and how awesome I was, too.

And now I was about to blow everything sky-high by telling my parents that the whole thing had been a giant fake.

"Mom, Dad—can I talk to you?" My mouth was made of flannel, my tongue too dry to generate sound. "It's about the Positive Action Group. I started it—that part wasn't a lie. But it wasn't like I let you guys believe."

I was determined to spill my guts. I was going to confess that the P.A.G. had never been a way to get involved for real, but a scam to make it look that way. I'd lay out how Mr. Fan-jet had gotten wind of it, and had turned it into an actual club, and suddenly kids were coming out of the woodwork to join up. I would explain the part where we got famous because of Audra Klincker and everybody in school wanted to be a pagger. I'd tell them about the mystery hacker who took over the web page. And I'd give them the unhappy ending, where we got shut down for what the Friends of Fuzzy did, and the only pagger who didn't mind was me, and now I was in trouble because the mystery hacker wasn't stopping.

The only part I'd leave out was the worst part, because I didn't want to think about it—that I was pretty sure the hacker was Pavel, and that I was fighting with my two best friends.

It would be a long speech for me, probably the most I'd ever spoken not into a headset. And the consequences would be huge: *You're banned from video games; you're grounded for life; you're being sent to Devil's Island; you'll be hanged by the neck until dead, dead, dead!*

But—why weren't they paying attention to me? Didn't they realize I was about to tell all?

"Are you guys even listening?"

"Of course, Cam." My mother was pale and tired. "We're just a little distracted, that's all. You've probably heard that the state is taking down our freeway ramp on Saturday. It's not good news for the store."

It was like my eyes were opening for the first time. Here they were, struggling to keep a family business afloat when everything was going wrong for them. They were putting in fourteen-hour days at work and worrying about where customers were going to come from when the main highway dropped everyone off at the mall. Was it any surprise that my problems weren't exactly uppermost in their minds?

"Anyway." My dad sighed. "We've got some big decisions ahead of us. We'll probably have to downsize the showroom. It might even make sense to try to sell it if we can find a buyer. Sorry, Cam. We've got a lot going on."

As terrible as I felt for their worries and their troubles, I couldn't keep the thought from bubbling to the surface: *I'm in the clear.* Of course, Dr. LaPierre was going to call one of these days. But he was going to accuse me of the website thing, and I was innocent of that.

No.

No more ducking and dodging. Mom and Dad deserved the truth. Maybe they were too stressed out to process it now. But even if everything went bad and they lost their store and had to put our lives back together again, sooner or later there would come a time when they had the right to know.

Okay, I'd write them a letter. When something was right there in black and white, it couldn't be ignored. And if it didn't sink in today, the message would still be there tomorrow, or the next day, or the day after that.

Wouldn't you know it—there wasn't a single blank piece of paper anywhere in my book bag or my room. I usually did my homework on my computer and turned it in online. It was Melody who wrote everything out in beautiful, flowing cursive. Barf.

Melody wouldn't grudge me a sheet of paper. Actually, Melody would grudge me the blood to keep my heart pumping, but she was at Katrina's right now. I went into her room and began opening desk drawers. The first was full of barrettes in a million colors, shapes, and sizes. The second contained pencils with erasers shaped like butterflies, ladybugs, and kittens. As I pulled out the third, a notebook caught my eye, its first page folded over.

There were words and numbers on it, everything in that girlie script of hers. For some reason, they rang a bell with me even though they didn't make any sense.

And then a bolt of recognition went through me like a shot from a plasma-based weapon.

The codes—the passwords for the P.A.G. web page and the Sycamore Middle School site!

Suddenly, my legs wouldn't support me, and I sat down cross-legged on the aquamarine carpet in her room.

The mystery hacker who'd called all those extra meetings—who'd created Pajama Day and Crazy Hat Day, and had everybody raising money selling Pagger Pizza. Who had rebuilt the P.A.G. page and was filling it with rebellious messages even after the school had taken it down. That shadowy computer jock had never been Pavel.

It was my own sister.

Confusion filled me up like helium in a balloon. Why? Why would she do this? What was in it for her? She'd never been one of those red-hot paggers who couldn't live unless they were oozing good deeds all over the place. And anyway, those messages on the web page had started even *before* the P.A.G. had gone big-time. What was her angle?

When the answer came to me, the helium turned to rage, lifting me up to hit the ceiling. What was in it for Melody? Absolutely nothing. She did it just to stick it to me. She'd figured out why I started the P.A.G. and she despised me so much that she deliberately turned my life upside down so she could sit on the sidelines and enjoy watching me squirm.

Well, it wouldn't work!

But as soon as that thought crossed my mind, I realized how wrong it was. It was working already. I was stressed to the point where I saw disaster around every corner; I couldn't play video games and didn't even want to; I'd practically given up on Rule the World. Worst of all, I'd chased my two best friends away. And my lifestyle? I had no life—period.

So it *had* worked. Score one for Melody. But she wasn't going to get away with it.

I used our new front door for the first time then, barreling out into a clammy drizzle. I barely noticed the weather. I was like a heat-seeking missile, and my guidance system had one target: Katrina's house. I covered the five blocks in record time

I stomped onto the porch, a man with a mission. I'd probably hit the doorbell fifteen times when Mrs. Bundy appeared, an annoyed expression on her face.

"All right, all right. I'm moving as fast as I—" Her anger softened when she recognized me. "Cam—hi. We're so sorry about what happened to the P.A.G."

Another thing—adults were treating me like I'd suffered a death in the family. I'd been sort of grooving on the extra kindness and understanding. Teachers hassled me less over long bathroom breaks, and Mrs. Backward gave me free candy at Sweetness and Light. Even our letter carrier made sure my gaming magazines didn't get crumpled in our mailbox. His seventh-grade son was a former pagger.

Now, though, I cut off Mrs. Bundy before she could start asking about my feelings. "Is my sister here?"

A sympathetic smile. "She's with Katrina in her room. Go on up."

She didn't even make me wipe my wet sneakers. I wiped them anyway. I no longer wanted special privileges because of my connection with the Positive Action Group. I wished I'd never thought of those three words.

I climbed the stairs and paused at the door, where a Star Wars poster declared *May the Force Be with All Who Enter Here*. Ha—the Force was nothing compared to what I was about to unleash on my rotten sister.

As I burst into the room, a deep voice declared *"Prepare for battle!"* and that was when I saw them. The girls were in front of the TV, gaming. Katrina wore a regular microphone, but Melody's was a shiny black helmet that completely covered her face.

She spoke: *"The Force is strong with you, young Jedi, but you will be annihilated!"*

The voice that came out wasn't Melody's. It wasn't even close. It was the low, rich, breathless bass of Darth Vader.

I nearly fainted on the spot.

Not only was Melody the hacker who was ruining my life on the P.A.G. web page; she was also the rogue gamer who'd been hounding me for months on the network— following me, challenging me, owning me.

Evil McKillPeople of Toronto, Canada, wasn't from Canada at all. She was from my house, up the stairs, second door to the left.

If I didn't drop dead right there on Katrina's Imperial Snow Walker carpet, I was going to live forever. There used to be a time when the world made sense—when video games were important, and a guy could live his life the way he wanted. But that was long, long ago, in a galaxy far, far away. Now up was down, black was white, and the only thing anybody cared about was a club that wasn't supposed to exist in the first place. You couldn't depend on friends or parents, and definitely not sisters. Even something as solid as a freeway ramp might not be there the next time you looked. So what could you depend on? Just this—that there would always be someone to throw an alien disrupter grenade into your plans.

Katrina noticed me first. Her reaction was to pull the Darth Vader voice-synthesizer helmet off her friend's head. I at least had the satisfaction of watching Melody turn green when she saw me standing there.

"Hey, Cam," she managed.

"Mom and Dad need you at home," I gritted through clenched teeth. "Right now."

It was a miracle I wasn't yelling at the top of my lungs. That lasted about three steps past the Bundys' front porch. I unloaded on her—not just about Evil McKillPeople, but the web-page thing, too. All the quiet I'd managed before was out the window now. I was amazed streetlights weren't exploding and satellites weren't dropping out of orbit from the sheer volume of my fury. They probably heard me on the Death Star.

"How did I ever hurt you?" I raved. "What terrible crime did I commit that I deserved this? What did I do to you to make you hate me so much that you would devote your whole life to wrecking everything I care about?"

She had looked pretty scared while I was going off on her, but when she turned on me, her face was full of anger. "Seriously? What did *you* ever do to *me*? Try being a second-class citizen in your own family! Try watching your brother bamboozle your parents so our whole house can revolve around your dumb lifestyle! Try being such a nobody in your own home that you have to go to your friend's house just to play a lousy video game."

"I let you play," I defended myself.

"Oh, sure—between four thirty and five a.m. on Tuesdays and alternate Thursdays! I moved a sofa cushion, and you blamed me for throwing off your aim!"

"You have no clue what it takes to game at a high level!" I accused.

"No," she agreed. "I know nothing about it. I'm just the person who beats you *every single time*! I'm onto you,

Cam Boxer. You're not mad because I'm Evil McKillPeople. You're mad because Evil McKillPeople is *better* than you!"

"You're not better than me!" I stammered. "It's just that—the Darth Vader voice throws me off . . ." But she had me there. I'd never gotten the best of Evil McKillPeople. He—*she*—was a master who had grown up and surpassed me under my very nose.

"Well, what about the web page, huh?" I ranted. "You don't care about the P.A.G. You never did. You figured out why I started the whole thing, and hacked into it just to stick it to me—so I'd get in trouble with Mom and Dad! And you're *still* doing it so I'll get in trouble at school, too!"

"You're right," she admitted, a little shamefaced. "It bothered me that Mom and Dad thought you were this big do-gooder when the whole thing was baloney. I wanted to make you suffer for it. And I thought it was funny when Mr. Fanshaw took over and turned the P.A.G. into a real club. But you know what? It only *started* as a goof. Once I saw how awesome it could be, I was on board just like everybody else. We helped *so* many people—and we helped ourselves at the same time. Everybody talks about school spirit, but all they mean is pep rallies and go-team-go! The P.A.G.—*that* was school spirit! Ask anybody who was in it. They'll tell you how great it was."

I thought of Xavier and his salsa bowl—currently full of Doritos, going stale and gathering dust in our basement. "Don't I count?" I asked bitterly. "It wasn't great for *me*."

She shook her head. "You're such an idiot, Cam. You're ticked off about the web page when should be down on your knees thanking me for helping to take the P.A.G. to the next level. Why, at its peak, you could have snapped your fingers and mobilized an army hundreds strong, ready to do anything you wanted them to. How many kids ever get that kind of power?"

"Power has no place in my lifestyle."

"Well, maybe it should," she retorted. "A little power would be a nice change in our house while we watch our parents' business—and the whole town—go down the drain."

"Like I could ever do anything about that," I said unhappily. "Even if the P.A.G. wasn't history and . . ." My voice trailed off.

Okay, the P.A.G. was over. But I thought of all those kids who'd come up to me to say how sorry they were, and how angry they were that we'd been blamed for something we didn't do. The phone calls and text messages; the notes jammed in my locker. The defiant comments that appeared on the illegal web page faster than the school could take them down.

We were standing stock-still in the middle of the road, Melody looking anxiously into my face. "What is it, Cam?"

"The P.A.G. is gone," I managed. "But we might still have the army."

CHAPTER TWENTY-EIGHT
CHUCK KINSEY

I never thought I'd love the P.A.G. as much as I did, or miss it as much as I was missing it now.

Then again, a lot of things were happening that I never thought could happen, like the Awesome Threesome not being friends anymore. That was so bad that Pavel and I could barely gag down our gummy worms. *We* were still friends, at least, but that was just a twosome. And not having Cam took the awesomeness out of everything.

Even Mrs. Backward could tell that something was wrong. "Melancholy, you boys are. Your friend is where?"

"We're kind of fighting," Pavel told her unhappily.

"Time, give him," she advised us in her backward language that Pavel and Cam understood, but always took me a little longer. "Work out, it will." Her brow clouded. "Our freeway ramp, not so much. The Transportation Department—hemorrhoids I wish on them!"

We still saw Cam at school, but he didn't talk to us and we didn't talk to him. He was keeping his distance, using his secret locker full-time because it was on the opposite side of the building from ours. I didn't tell Pavel, but I even went online a few times just to check if Cam was on the gaming network. I never found him, not once. If there was anything weirder than the Awesome Threesome breaking up, it was Cam not playing video games.

Pavel was as sad as I was, but also pretty sore. "He deserves it. Where does he get off accusing me of messing with the web page?"

Speaking of the web page, it was back up again. At least, sometimes it was. One minute it would be there like before, filled with angry words and challenges like *PAGGERS FIGHT BACK* and *DR. LAPIERRE UNFAIR* and *AXE FUZZY, NOT THE GOOD GUYS*. But just a few minutes later, it was gone again. I couldn't figure out what was going on.

"It's no big mystery," Pavel told me. "Some pagger's hacking into the site and putting the page back up. And the school keeps taking it down."

I looked deep into his face. "But are you the pagger who's hacking in?"

He glared at me. "Don't *you* start. It wasn't me before and it isn't me now."

I must have seemed disappointed. The truth was, I *liked* what it said on the web page. I was ready to fight for the P.A.G. But because the page would only be there for a few minutes, there was never time to put in any information. Nothing about where to go, or what to do, or who to talk to.

Every morning while I ate breakfast, I'd check it on my iPad, hoping against hope for word that the P.A.G. might be getting back together again.

And then, one day, there it was:

IT'S TIME TO MAKE A STAND!
BIG MEETING — 3:15 TODAY

"But where?" I almost shouted into my cornflakes. Desperately, I tried scrolling down for more details. That was when the page tried to refresh itself, flickered once, and disappeared.

I called Pavel.

"I saw it, too," he confirmed. "We'll just have to ask around when we get to school. Somebody must know what's going on."

He was half right. At school everyone was buzzing about the latest post. I guess we weren't the only ex-paggers following the on-again, off-again page. The problem was that nobody knew where this big meeting was going to be held.

"Well, that makes sense," Pavel reasoned. "The school is monitoring this. If they give the location, the first guy to show up will be Dr. LaPierre."

It didn't make me feel any better. "Yeah, but it's not going to be much of a meeting if nobody knows where to go!"

Rumors started flying. It would be the gym, where all our meetings took place. The guidance department, since Mr. Fanshaw was our faculty adviser. The hallway outside Dr. LaPierre's office, just to show him who was boss. The football stadium—close to school, but away from the teachers' prying eyes.

Some kids even thought the Boxer home would be the spot. Only Pavel and I knew how wrong that was. Nobody cared less about the P.A.G. than Cam himself.

I'll bet our school shattered the world record for cell phone write-ups that day. Everyone was on the school site, hoping for more information from the phantom P.A.G. page. You could hear the *"Ahhhhh!"* from every hall in the school when it suddenly reappeared just a few seconds after the three o'clock bell.

I stared at my phone's small screen:

MEETING PLACE:
WHERE IT ALL BEGAN

A buzz of confusion rose. Where it all began? What was that supposed to mean?

"I've got it!" crowed String's voice in sudden triumph. "This must mean the playing field at the elementary school where The String scored his first touchdown!"

There was a general sigh of letdown. I liked String, but his suggestion made about as much sense as everything else he said.

"The P.A.G. started in Cam's basement," I mused to Pavel. "Or maybe at your house, where you set up the web page."

He shook his head. "The only people who know about that are us and Cam. And there's no way he has anything to do with this. I thought of the music room, where the P.A.G. first met—but we'd never fit in there now. No, 'where it all began' can only mean where we did our first good deed—the senior citizens' garden project."

We told as many paggers as we could, hoping that they would spread the word from there. But obviously we weren't the only ones who remembered that great day when the P.A.G. changed from a club on paper to a real force for good in Sycamore. As we made our way across town toward Seventh Street, there were already a lot of kids ahead of us. The trickle turned to a stream, and pretty soon, the sidewalk was so jammed that a lot of walkers spilled over into the road, slowing traffic.

The closer we got, the greater the excitement level, the louder the chatter. I was feeling it as much as anyone.

The fact that the P.A.G. was coming back to life awakened something in me, too. Not that we weren't still shut down officially. But there was something more to us, something Dr. LaPierre couldn't touch. And neither could the Friends of Fuzzy.

"Who do you think is doing this?" I asked Pavel. "It can't be Mr. Fanshaw. He could get fired."

Pavel shrugged. "We'll know soon enough."

We crossed the street and entered the garden. It wasn't the whole P.A.G., but there had to be at least two hundred of us there, clustered around about ten kids at the center of the now frost-covered garden. I saw Xavier first—he was hard to miss. There were school co-presidents Jordan and Kelly, along with Felicia, the campaign manager, even though there was no campaign anymore. And—was that Daphne?

"I sure hope they brought a megaphone," Pavel commented. "Listen to this crowd. We're not going to hear a word."

That turned out to be one of the rare times the great Pavel was wrong about something. As soon as Xavier held up his hands for order, all those paggers got real silent real fast. Then he squatted down, and for a minute I thought we'd come all this way to watch a former juvenile delinquent do knee bends. But no—he was hunkering down to boost somebody up onto his shoulders.

"That's *Cam*!" Pavel blurted.

When everybody recognized the P.A.G.'s founder, the senior citizens' garden project went berserk for five full minutes.

As soon as things quieted down again, Cam began to talk. "We helped a lot of people." He didn't even raise his voice, but we hung on his every word. "Now we have a chance to help ourselves. We have a chance to help the whole town."

Pavel and I exchanged an astonished look. No one hated public speaking more than Cam. He was always telling us that it didn't fit into his lifestyle. What was going on here?

"On Saturday morning," Cam went on, "the Division of Highways is going to knock down our exit ramp, and everybody thinks there's nothing we can do about it. But what the P.A.G. taught us is there's *never* nothing we can do. If we could get hundreds of people to pick up garbage, we can get hundreds of people to stand on our ramp and block the demolition crew."

I turned to Pavel. "That can't work. Can it?"

He seemed stunned. "It's so obvious. I can't believe nobody thought of it before!"

"Yeah, but people aren't stronger than bulldozers."

"In a way they are," he countered. "A highway crew's not allowed to plow over human beings. If we pack that ramp and refuse to move, there's nothing they can do!"

I was blown away. My parents, their friends, Mrs. Backward, the city council, the mayor, every adult in town was mourning over the loss of this freeway ramp. And the only person to come up with a plan was an eighth grader. And not just any eighth grader—Cam Boxer, the world's greatest natural slacker!

"Maybe the school shut us down," Cam concluded. "But that doesn't mean we can't be the Positive Action Group in our spare time. I think we've got one more good deed in us. And this one's the most important of all."

There was a low, thoughtful murmur as the audience chewed over Cam's words. And when it began to sink in that this was something that could work, the hum swelled to a roar. We could *do* this! If we got a big enough turnout, we could stop those bulldozers. And for the P.A.G., bringing together hundreds of volunteers was something that used to happen two or three times a week!

The crowd rushed toward Cam, and Pavel and I rushed with them. The P.A.G. president teetered atop Xavier's strong shoulders, reaching down to slap high fives.

Pavel was pink with exhilaration. "Cam was awesome! And not a word about aliens or his clan or Rule the World!"

I nodded happily. "Let's go congratulate him!"

That was easier said than done. Everybody wanted a piece of Cam right then. He was the man of the hour, the star of the moment.

We shoved our way forward until we were as close as we could get in the mob.

"Hey, Cam!" I called, waving.

"Over here!" Pavel added.

The P.A.G. president's eyes panned the crowd, passing right over us.

CHAPTER TWENTY-NINE
DAPHNE LEIBOWITZ

I still loved Elvis. There was no question about that. And I was still worried sick about him.

But facts were facts, and it was time to face up to a tough one: Elvis wouldn't be showing his buckteeth around Sycamore anymore. No one had seen him since painting day at the Y. He had moved on. Or worse.

I didn't want to think about "or worse."

Like it or not, I had to be mature and accept reality. The P.A.G. was back and Elvis wasn't. And the P.A.G. was *good*—great, even. What could be better than helping— even if the list of who we helped didn't include a certain beaver.

Anyway, even Elvis wasn't as important as saving our freeway ramp and maybe our whole town. Cam was right about that.

By Friday, every single kid at Sycamore Middle School knew the drill for early Saturday. At seven a.m., we were all going to meet at the freeway. We would stand on it, around it, and in front of it, and block the wrecking crew from getting anywhere near it.

Cam had only one rule for us: We had to keep it a

secret. Mostly from our parents, who might think that taking on a bulldozer was a bad idea. Parents could be like that sometimes—getting obsessed over a couple of details and not seeing the big picture.

I took that rule really seriously when I snuck out of the house early Saturday, closing my bedroom door so my folks would think I was sleeping late. Outside, it was cold and clear, the sun a big fireball on the horizon. I'd deliberately left my bike hidden in the bushes so I wouldn't make noise getting it out of the garage. I was meeting up with Cam, Melody, and Katrina for the ride over to the freeway.

I figured I'd have to wait for them, but they were already there, checking their watches impatiently. Dark circles ringed the bloodshot eyes of the P.A.G. president. The responsibility of today must have really been weighing on him. The girls greeted me, but all he said was, "I can't believe the sun's up at this hour."

Melody seemed nervous. "I sure hope we're not the only ones crazy enough to do this."

"Are you kidding?" Katrina crowed. "I pity the poor bulldozer that tries to get past the P.A.G."

As we pedaled south toward the highway, kids began to appear on the streets around us—on bicycles, Rollerblades, scooters, skateboards, and on foot.

"Looks like it's going to be a good turnout," I commented.

Cam didn't answer. He was really in the zone. Either that or he wasn't completely awake.

As we moved along, the steadily growing stream of paggers began to converge on the main roads heading into downtown. There were waves and subdued greetings, but no one wanted to attract attention and give away our plans. I recognized String skateboarding with some teammates, and Jordan, Kelly, and Felicia on bikes. Xavier was among the walkers, his long strides keeping pace with the rest of us. I'd never seen him so serious.

Katrina looked around. "I'm kind of surprised there are so many cars out so early."

She was right. It wasn't exactly a traffic jam, but a surprising number of motorists were out for six forty a.m. on a weekend. And all of them seemed to be heading the same way we were.

Melody's brow furrowed. "You don't think a bunch of paggers got lazy and asked their parents for a lift?"

That got Cam's attention. He began peering into windows as the vehicles cruised by. "Teenagers!"

I frowned. "Don't they sleep in even later than everybody else?"

"Don't you get it?" he rasped. "It's the Friends of Fuzzy!

They must have found out what we're doing and they're trying to beat us to it and steal the credit!"

"Let them," Melody reasoned. "As long as it stops the bulldozers, who gets credit shouldn't matter."

"You don't know the Fuzzies! They're crazy!" He glanced over his shoulder and went suddenly white. *"Evasive action!"*

"This isn't a video game," Melody began.

Then I saw it, too—a bright red Dodge Charger, right on our tail and gaining fast. The four of us swerved to the right and jolted up onto the sidewalk. The big sedan roared past, its window open and none other than Jennifer Del Rio hanging out, her long dark hair wild in the wind. She shook her fist and shouted, "This'll teach you to mess with Farley J. Peachfuzz!"

Her boyfriend stomped on the accelerator to leave us in the dust, and that was when it happened. A blur of brown fur hustled out into the road from behind a bush. The Charger braked and swerved, but it was too late.

Thump!

The right fender struck a glancing blow and sent the unlucky animal skittering back to the curb.

My eyes got so wide I thought they'd suck in the rest of my face. A horrified scream was torn from my throat.

"Elvis!"

"No way!" blurted Cam.

I was off my bike even before Elvis had stopped rolling. All I could think of was that the poor little guy was dead, and it was our fault. If we'd been quick enough to catch him that day at the Y, we could have put him in his new habitat. And he would have been so happy that he never would have run out in front of a speeding car.

He wasn't moving. My eyes blurred with tears. I reached for him, determined that his last experience in life would be love.

He slapped my hand away with his tail, scuttled across the sidewalk, and disappeared through the tall grass into the woods.

CHAPTER THIRTY
JENNIFER DEL RIO

Give the middle school kids credit. They almost pulled it off.

We didn't know until last night what they were planning at the freeway ramp. Joel Osterman's seventh-grade sister accidentally ate a peanut, and Benadryl is like truth serum for her. She blabbed the whole thing.

I had to admit it. It was an amazing idea—better than anything I could have come up with. It would have lifted the Positive Action Group out of the toilet and made them legends in this town.

So of course I had to steal it. It would be easy for us. We had one huge advantage over the little kids: We could drive. All I had to do was sound the alert—a group text here, a tweet there, a posting or two on the Friends of Fuzzy Facebook page. Cam Boxer would never know what hit him.

And now, a bonus: Not only were we going to save the freeway ramp. We were going to save the beaver, too.

"I don't get it, Jen," Tony panted, running behind me through the trees. "I thought we were stopping bulldozers."

"That's still on," I tossed over my shoulder. "But first we're going to rescue that beaver. He can't be hard to catch after you winged him with the car."

Tony sounded rueful. "I didn't mean for that to happen. What if he's really hurt?"

"Not our problem. He's going in his habitat, dead or alive!"

I could hear the middle schoolers crashing through the underbrush behind us. I recognized Boxer and that crazy girl from the Y pool, but not the other two. They looked younger—sixth graders, maybe.

That was the only thing that could sink us—the chance that one of them might get to the rodent before we did. There were four of them and only two of us.

Not missing a step, I whipped out my phone and dialed Sarah Schusselberg, First Assistant Grand Pal of the Friends of Fuzzy.

"We're just passing through downtown," Sarah reported. "Jen, have you see all these kids? It looks like the whole middle school's going to show up!"

"Never mind that," I puffed. "We just had a beaver sighting."

Sarah was all business. "Location?"

"Ravine Park. I think we're behind Taco Hut right now, but you can't depend on that, because we're moving pretty fast. And we've got company. The Boxer kid, for one. And that nut job from the pool."

"I'll spread the word," she promised.

The crazy girl was screaming down the forest. *"Elvis!"* She had a loud voice that was like a cheese grater against my brain. *"Elvis, come back!"*

"Will you shut up?" I barked back at her. "If he hears you, he won't come back! He'll run a mile!"

A streak of brown fur flashed through the underbrush before me. But before I could react, the two younger girls dashed past me. Who knew sixth graders could be so fast?

"Tony!" I snapped.

"I'm on it!" He took three giant strides, tripped on a root, and landed flat on his face. Those clunky black boots looked cool with his leather jacket, but maybe they weren't so great for a beaver hunt.

Our quarry scrambled through some tall grass and took cover among the thick leaves of a fallen tree limb. I caught up with the girls, squeezed my bigger body between them, and kicked away the branch. Behind it cowered a terrified woodchuck. False alarm.

"There he goes!" called Cam behind me, which started the crazy one screeching again.

I hauled Tony to his feet and started after Cam.

He tried to hold me back. "Come on, Jen. You're a presidential scholar, head cheerleader, in more clubs than anyone in the history of Sycamore High. This time next year, you'll be at *Harvard*! Do you really have to go to war over a beaver?"

I pulled free of him. "I'm not at Harvard *yet*!" I exploded. "We need that rodent!"

At that moment, Sarah came crashing through the woods, followed by a pack of high schoolers. The cavalry!

"I dressed for a freeway ramp, not a forest," Sarah complained, zipping her cashmere hoodie up to her neck.

"Follow me!" I ordered, leading the charge after the little kids.

It was easy enough to follow them. The nut job was wailing like a police siren. What was she? Elvis's mother?

Sarah did a good job spreading the word; pretty soon the Friends of Fuzzy were all over the place. We needed as many searchers as we could get, since a beaver was low and built for hiding in the underbrush.

I was reaching to pull my right sneaker out of a patch of mud when I bumped heads with a kid who was easily five years younger than me. A middle schooler, definitely, but not one of the original four.

"How did you get here?" I rasped.

"I just followed everybody else," he replied. "Don't you know Elvis is in the woods somewhere?"

That was when I looked closely at the many faces peering behind trees and into underbrush. Yeah, the woods teemed with kids searching for the beaver. But at least half of them were from the middle school!

It was like the YMCA all over again—Friends of Fuzzy versus P.A.G. Except this time, there was no way to blame the whole thing on them and walk away heroes. Today, the only victor would be whoever emerged from these woods carrying the beaver.

It wasn't a battle, exactly. But when you had hundreds of people stumbling around a maze of trees and vegetation, things were bound to get ugly. Every squirrel and jackrabbit caused a stampede. Kids from both schools went down, sliding in mud, tripped up by vines, and knocked silly by low branches. Some tumbled over an embankment into a creek, leaving them soaked and shivering, their phones ruined.

Sarah wound up at the bottom of a hole, and had to be hauled out by the wrestling team. Robby Michaels got his jeans caught on a branch and ripped his pants clean off. One of the middle schoolers climbed a tree for a better view and couldn't get himself down. That drew a whole crowd, shouting instructions.

I was so distracted by those idiots that I almost missed it—a high-pitched whining sound, almost like a crying baby.

What would a baby be doing in the middle of the woods?

I took a tentative step in the direction of the noise, and there he was, huddled in a thicket of juniper. It was definitely him—big rodent head; brown fur; broad, flat tail.

The beaver!

I approached in slow motion, savoring the moment, visions of Harvard Yard dancing in my head. Squatting low, I reached out to grab the little animal from behind.

"*El-vis!*"

Just as my hands closed on the furry hind legs, the nut job came careening into the thicket, grabbing the beaver from the front. For an instant, we froze in pure shock. Then the two of us hauled him clear of the bushes and stood toe-to-toe, staring belligerently at each other.

"He's mine!" I growled over the crying baby sound.

"He needs to see a vet!" she exclaimed urgently. "He got hit by a car!"

"I know that," I retorted. "I was in the car that hit him."

"He's injured! He's barely resisting us!"

"The Friends of Fuzzy rescued this beaver," I said through clenched teeth. "Once we get credit for that, he's all yours and good riddance. Now let go!"

I yanked hard. The beaver squealed, but the crazy girl held on. I felt a warm trickle on my hands.

He peed on me!

No one peed on Jennifer Del Rio. I had a list in my mind of all the things I would never tolerate, and this was right near the top.

"*Tony!*" I howled.

The crazy girl started screaming, "*Cam!*"

Well, that did it. The ground shook as every kid in the woods converged on the sound of our yelling and the beaver's cries. Even the guy who was stuck in the tree got himself down somehow to see what was going on.

Tony pushed his way through the crowd to stand beside me. The Boxer kid took his place next to the crazy girl.

"Tony," I raged, barely able to speak. "This is my beaver! I'm the one he peed on, and he's mine!"

Tears were streaming down the nut job's face. "You can have him," she quavered. "Just don't pull him anymore. You're hurting him, and he's scared. And you have to promise to take him to a vet. I'll let go when you do that."

"I'm not promising anything!" I spat. "I'm taking him straight to Audra Klincker's house so that everybody knows the Friends of Fuzzy are heroes!"

And then Tony, *my* boyfriend, who was supposed to support me, said a single word: "No."

"No? What do you mean 'no'?"

I'd never heard his voice so gentle—or so insistent. "Give her the beaver, Jen."

"But—" I sputtered. "Harvard—"

"If Harvard needs this beaver so much, maybe you should pick another school," Tony said quietly.

There we were, the crazy girl and me, surrounded by practically every kid in Sycamore, locked in the ultimate standoff. And suddenly, the nut job let go and placed Elvis into my arms. She even took off her jacket and wrapped him up for me.

I had absolutely no idea what to do or say. She loved him that much that she was willing to *lose*—in front of everybody she knew—just to keep him safe. It was the most surprising thing I'd ever seen. Maybe next year, at Harvard, one of the professors would be able to explain it to me.

A few of the kids—from both schools—started clapping.

Over that sound swelled another, louder noise. It was the grinding roar of heavy machinery.

Cam was the first to recognize it. "The bulldozers!"

CHAPTER THIRTY-ONE
CAMERON BOXER

"Oh, man!" I moaned. "We were so worried about saving the beaver that we forgot about saving the ramp!"

"The freeway's just on the other side of the woods!" Tony exclaimed excitedly. *"Run!"*

I'd seen some pretty insane things in video games—battle scenes with bullets chirping past my ears; car races so realistic you could almost feel the hot blast of exploding fuel tanks; full-on attacks by cannibals, zombies, aliens, and werewolves; the sickening crunch of an entire planet sucked down a black hole.

It was nothing compared to the sight of hundreds of kids pounding through the woods in a desperate sprint to make it to the freeway before the bulldozers. We ran flat out, underbrush grabbing our ankles and branches scratching painfully at our faces. We left behind our bikes and skateboards and scooters. The high schoolers abandoned their cars. Nobody thought twice about it. The only thing that mattered was making it to our ramp in time to stop the demolition.

Part of me was thinking: *This isn't you! You belong on a couch in front of a screen! You shouldn't be blundering through woods, dodging trees and hurdling bushes. Your only physical strain should be your fingers on a controller! This is crazy!*

And it *was* crazy. I had no breath, my eyes stung from dripping sweat, my lungs burned with every stride, and I was sure my heart rate had climbed higher than my usual maximum of sixty. But I was running faster than anybody—except maybe String, who was out in front of the pack, bellowing, "Hang in there! The String is coming!"

I passed Jennifer, who was stumbling along carrying Elvis, and Daphne, who was keeping pace, shouting "Don't drop him!" I passed Jordan, Kelly, and Felicia, and a little farther ahead, Melody and Katrina. I even passed Xavier, who was galloping full tilt, his huge body bent forward into the wind, his face glistening with perspiration.

Not far behind the leaders, I pulled even with Pavel and Chuck. Running at top speed over rough ground wasn't exactly the place for a conversation, but they both nodded in my direction when they saw me.

"Gotta get there," I gasped.

"Gotta do it," Chuck managed, panting.

"Gotta," Pavel agreed.

It was all the breath any of us could spare.

Then, amazingly, we began to gain on the leaders— String and some of the high school track stars. Unbelievable. We weren't athletes; we were gamers, couch potatoes. Yet today we were the Awesome Threesome in a totally new way—the fastest kids in Sycamore.

When we broke out of the trees, it was sudden and unexpected, almost like a giant curtain had been swept aside to let us through. The sight that met our eyes stopped us dead in our tracks, and we were almost trampled by the herd thundering up behind us.

There was the demolition crew from the Division of Highways—hard hats, jackhammers, bulldozers, front loaders, and dump trucks to haul away the rubble of what used to be the gateway to our town. There was the ramp, waiting to be demolished.

But they couldn't get to it.

Blocking their way were our parents, our teachers, storekeepers, doctors, lawyers, businesspeople, mail carriers, waitresses, and short-order cooks. They were packed onto the ramp, and in front of it on the service road. Mayor Dolinka was there, the town council, Audra Klincker, Mrs. Backward, the head librarian, Dr. LaPierre, Mr. Fan-club, even . . .

"Mom and Dad?" Melody blurted, pulling up beside me. "Did you tell them about this?"

I shook my head in wonder. "Not me."

Pavel had a theory. "A few kids must have blabbed. Or they got caught sneaking out and spilled the beans. And the word just spread."

Amazing. Every kid in Sycamore went off chasing after Elvis and forgot to save our exit. But it was okay because every adult in Sycamore showed up to save the exit for us.

We all squeezed onto the ramp, and believe me, it was a miracle we didn't demolish it ourselves—that's how many of us were jammed on there. Melody and I pushed over to stand with Mom and Dad.

"I can't believe you guys are here!" Melody told them over the noise of the crowd and the heavy machinery.

"Our exit would have been toast without you!" I added. "Thanks!"

"We're the ones who should be thanking you," my dad said emotionally. "We were so wound up in what was happening to our business that it never even occurred to us to try to do something about it. It took you kids to show us that."

"It took your Positive Action Group," Mom added to me.

"I don't really deserve all the credit for what the P.A.G. does," I admitted. "Today is something Melody and I kind of came up with together."

It was almost like we were holding the Fourth of July on a little strip of pavement. Kids were hanging out with their families. Neighbors were meeting and greeting. Everything was there except the hot dogs. But it was really tense, too, because the whole party was happening in front of enough heavy machinery to plow us under in about fifteen seconds. The foreman of the demolition crew was shouting into his cell phone, asking for instructions, while the workers leaned on shovels and jackhammers, glaring at us.

Time ticked by, and before we knew it, it wasn't morning anymore. The workers turned off the trucks and bulldozers. We smelled victory and got really excited, but they were only breaking for lunch. A few of the restaurant employees got food for us, too, and both sides dug in to wait out the afternoon.

It was actually pretty dull, and I'm sure all the other kids thought so, too, and probably a lot of the adults. Still, for some reason, it never occurred to me to take out my phone and check on my clan. It wasn't fun, but it felt *big*. And the fact that the whole town was doing it together made it even bigger.

It happened just before two thirty. I was half-asleep from boredom and exhaustion, so when the crew started up the machinery again, I nearly jumped out of my skin. It was a scary moment. What if they started driving at us, superslow, inch by inch? Would we have to choose between backing away and getting run over?

Worried glances passed around the crowd. Would the workers actually do that? Surely they didn't want to hurt anybody. Dad shoved Melody and me behind him, although how he thought he could stop a bulldozer was beyond me. All around us, parents did the same with their own kids.

Then, one by one, the trucks, earthmovers, and loaders turned around and drove off down the freeway. We watched the line of road-busting equipment head out of sight. And when the last pickup disappeared from view, the celebration broke out.

It was pretty ill—everybody screaming and high-fiving and throwing their hats in the air. Kids who refused to be seen in public with their parents didn't mind being hugged and kissed in front of the whole town. We'd been victims for so long, watching the new mall suck the life out of Sycamore. Now we were back in charge of our own lives. Pavel, Chuck, and I pulled gummy worms out of our pockets and toasted the great moment.

I turned to Pavel, shame-faced. "I never should have accused you of messing with the web page."

"Technically understandable," Pavel mumbled, his mouth full of candy.

"Technically, maybe," I conceded. "But that's not Awesome Threesome style."

The only person not jumping for joy was Jennifer. She couldn't—she still had the injured Elvis, wrapped in Daphne's jacket, clutched in her arms. She was so determined to get credit for saving the beaver that she hadn't let go of him through all those hours. Now she was walking purposefully toward Audra Klincker, the reporter who would tell the world about the Friends of Fuzzy and their epic rescue.

But then something must have changed the head cheerleader's mind. In the middle of all the chaos, she walked right past the reporter and gave the injured animal to Dr. Casper, our town vet.

That might have been the most amazing thing to come from a pretty amazing day—finding out that Jennifer Del Rio had a heart.

CHAPTER THIRTY-TWO
DAPHNE LEIBOWITZ

It was the happiest of all happy endings.

I meant that Elvis turned out to be okay, not the part where the town was saved. That was pretty good, too.

But back to Elvis. Picture the best fireworks display you've ever seen against a pitch-black sky, during a supernova, with Mount Krakatoa erupting in the background.

That still doesn't come close to describing how thrilled I was when Dr. Casper announced that Elvis was fine. After the celebration on the ramp, the vet took the poor beaver back to his office for a full examination. The diagnosis: only bruising, no internal damage. The car had sideswiped him, not hit him straight on. He was scared and shaken up, but otherwise in perfect beaver health.

As for the ramp, people were still a little nervous that the bulldozers might come back the next day, or the day after that. Just because we'd stopped them once didn't mean the state government had changed its mind. No way could everybody in Sycamore put their lives on hold to stand out by the freeway as human shields forever. But the next week we got word that the Transportation Department had postponed the demolition until they could "review" the situation. Mayor Dolinka told us that the state was so far behind in reviewing things that Sycamore was off the hook for at least three years. And since that was too long to leave a crumbling ramp, the Division of Highways would have to repair it. In other words, by the time anyone got around to demolishing our exit, it wouldn't need demolishing anymore.

It was good news, I guess, but it didn't exactly fill me with confidence in government. I knew *kids* who were this flaky, but the state was supposed to be reliable, right? How could we be sure they wouldn't just change their minds?

Cam wasn't worried. "If the bulldozers ever come back, the P.A.G. will go out and stand on the ramp again," he promised everybody.

That was the real big story. The Positive Action Group had been reinstated with Cam back as president. The minute that happened, every single kid who wasn't already a member joined up. Mr. Fanshaw said it had to be the first time in the history of school that a club ever reached 100 percent membership. Our first project was selling tickets for the Fall Charity Raffle. I wasn't convinced that was quite as important as some of the other things the P.A.G. could turn its attention to, but Mr. Fanshaw assured me that this was what Cam wanted. Well, how could I argue with that? If it hadn't been for Cam, who knew what would have become of poor Elvis?

After a few days under observation in Dr. Casper's veterinary clinic, Elvis was finally introduced into the habitat we had built for him all those weeks ago. He loved it, just like I'd always known he would. Watching him swim and play and chew wood filled me with so much happiness I was afraid I might cry. Okay, I did cry. Luckily, nobody noticed, because there was a lot going on right then.

Mayor Dolinka himself held an official town ceremony in the woods, and even unveiled a plaque that read:

ELVIS'S POND
A P.A.G. PROJECT

This didn't sit too well with Jennifer Del Rio and the Friends of Fuzzy, who weren't in love with the idea of the middle school getting all the credit. They had to suck it up, though. What choice did they have? Time was on *our* side, not theirs. In a couple of years, we would be them, and they would be gone.

In the end, what really mattered was that Elvis was safe and sound and happy. We had the P.A.G. to thank for that, which meant we had Cam to thank, too. He was the best thing that ever happened to this town. I can't believe I actually said that guy was a slacker.

Seriously, what was I thinking?

CHAPTER THIRTY-THREE
CAMERON BOXER

Rule the World was ill.

Beyond ill.

The convention hall stretched as far as the eye could see. Game logos the size of buildings hung everywhere. And the people—thousands of them, ages nine to ninety, some dressed as characters from their favorite games. It was my lifestyle poured out around me in all its natural beauty.

I wasn't totally relaxed, though. As I eyed the competition at the various tournament stations, it looked pretty fierce. I had my work cut out for me, no question about that.

My father kept me company while I waited for my partner to arrive. "Nervous?"

"Just excited," I replied. "I've been waiting for this day my whole life. I honestly didn't believe it would ever come."

"About that." Dad shuffled uncomfortably. "I had a crazy idea last week that you only started the P.A.G. because you were afraid we were going to take away your console. Mom and I are proud of everything you've accomplished these past months, but we'd hate to think that you're doing it just for us. So if you want to quit . . ."

"What?" I was stunned. "No way! I'm the pagger-in-chief! They *need* me!"

Hey, I wasn't abandoning my lifestyle. Still, when I looked around Rule the World—ill as it was—it wasn't *everything*. It wasn't my family, my friends, my school, my town. The Positive Action Group had worked its way into all that. It had started as a hoax, but had ended up the realest thing about me.

Besides, the P.A.G. had never needed me to run it anyway, so staying on as president wouldn't take a huge bite out of my lifestyle. Plus, there was no way I was leaving the Friends of Fuzzy to take credit for all the good deeds in town. The word around Sycamore was that Jennifer Del Rio had been accepted to Harvard. Poor Harvard.

"Hi, Cam!"

Chuck fist-bumped me. He'd made the trip to Rule the World just to cheer me on. What a great friend. It was hard to imagine we'd been fighting.

I'd never say it out loud, but I was glad he wasn't my partner for this tournament. The same went for Pavel, who was right behind him. He was every bit as good a gamer as Chuck, and supersmart besides. But the level of play around here was so intense that neither of them would have been able to handle it.

"Ready?" Pavel asked me.

"I will be in a minute."

We all watched as my mom approached, escorting my Rule the World partner. Melody came over to stand beside me.

"Got your game face on?"

I grinned. "You know me. It's the only face I've got."

That's right, my sister, Melody, was my partner—or maybe I should say I was *her* partner, since she was better than me. It was a little humbling to admit, but we were in the big leagues here, and the stakes had never been so high.

When you were facing Rule the World–level competition, you needed someone like Evil McKillPeople on your side.

About the Author

Gordon Korman is the #1 bestselling author of five books in The 39 Clues series as well as eight books in his Swindle series: *Swindle, Zoobreak, Framed, Showoff, Hideout, Jackpot, Unleashed,* and *Jingle.* His other books include *This Can't Be Happening at Macdonald Hall!* (published when he was fourteen); *The Toilet Paper Tigers; Radio Fifth Grade; Ungifted; Schooled;* the trilogies Island, Everest, Dive, Kidnapped, Titanic, and The Hypnotists; and the series On the Run. He lives in New York with his family.